Stories from

My

Heart

Nandini

i

Stories from

My

Heart

Nandini

By the same author

Fire in my Heart - A spiritual autobiography
ISBN 81 - 7525 -586 -2

Contents

Kiss of the Divine

Call of the Divine

Illustrations

The Kiss of the Divine

The Call of the Divine

All illustrations and photographs are by the author.

Acknowledgements

My thanks and sincere gratitude go to my husband, Godfrey for his enthusiasm and help in editing the script and to Julian Bewick for his technical assistance. Thanks to Swami Rama Sadhaka Grama for providing a tree that has housed so many species of birds all happily living together and for the cows that roamed in the field beside it.

Dedication

To all Lovers of the Divine

This work is humbly offered to the feet of my dearest spiritual brother, Swami Veda Bharati of the Swami Rama Sadhaka Grama, Rishikesh, who has loved and supported me throughout my life. (Even when I didn't know it) and who has provided the setting in which these stories were born.

KISS OF THE DIVINE

*The story
of a cow
and
a
white bird*

Nandini

Whilst sitting immersed in the bliss light

It all began very early one morning whilst sitting immersed in the bliss light of a waning moon and a solitary star. The cool presence of their luminosity kissed and embraced my being. The silence spoke tremendously of the importance of connections, of relationships and of unity within the great diversity. A bird sitting on a nearby rooftop opened her heart to that 'inner' music which is to be found only in the 'silence' of which I spoke earlier. She sang her song so divinely, so purely, that she became immersed in the light of her own radiance. Ahhh ... that sweetness so adorable to those whose hearts are open.

A story was unfolding:

Chapter One

It so happened that not very far away, on a little grassy corner of a dusty road, lived a cow. She spent her time quietly humming to herself. Her heart was open and contentment was engraved in her kind and gentle brown eyes. She knew her place in the great scheme of things, and most of all she knew she was loved deeply and totally by one small, slim and brilliant white, long-necked bird who had become intoxicated by her loving patient eyes and full heart. She also provided him with breakfast, lunch and supper with an occasional snack in between.

You may wonder how this could be. I shall tell you.

When Saffron (for that was her given name, due to the fact that her coat had a beautiful reddish sheen to it whenever the sun shone) was born, it was the end of the rainy season but the nights and early mornings were still chilly and damp. She was born in the warmth of an early March afternoon. Her place of birth was a patch of land near the River Ganges. This little plot of land was a fragrant haven with many little, sweet-scented flowers dotted amongst the wild grasses. It was surrounded by a dusty track for most of the year, but for now it was full of puddles and little rivulets of water as rain had fallen in great torrents just the night before.

'It was an omen; a blessing from the Great Divine Source.' thought Gaia.

Cow and egret: Saffron and Raji-B, Virbhadra, Rishikesh

Saffron's mother, Gaia had been a beautiful soft brown coloured cow with big, black eyes back in her youth, but now she was exhausted. She was really too old to be giving birth and she knew that her days were numbered. So with all the love she could muster, she fed and nurtured her little one until three weeks later, she died. Saffron cried and cried. She cried for so long that she did not take any nourishment or notice of anyone or anything until a youthful, white, long-necked bird came along.

A few days later, a small girl, playing along the roadside discovered the dead mother and the distraught little Saffron, ran to tell her parents, who immediately came to the rescue. They buried Mother Gaia and they took little Saffron to come and live outside their home which was just down the track from where she had been born. The young white bird moved along too.

The death of her mother had been a tragedy. Saffron had mourned her loss so completely, so utterly, that now she had found a certain sense of calm and peace in her mind and heart. She would never forget her mother's dying words whispered into her young ears. This was 'her' secret which would give her strength in the days to come. In fact these words were to be her solace to the end of her life.

Chapter Two

The sun set, the moon rose. The heavy rains had stopped. The days became warmer as they lengthened into the hot, humid and dusty summer. The white bird never left Saffron's side. Saffron came to love him deeply and there came a time when she felt that she could confide in him. The feelings were mutual.

Now, the young white bird had been blessed with devoted parents, and his aged grandfather from his mother's side had lived for a long time near the family nest. His grandfather had often sat beside him in his 'nesting' days, teaching him how to live in a wholesome and honest way: how to be *true* to his race and how to *share* when times were hard. Yes, he had learned much from his wise and beloved grandfather. There were many wonderful stories they had often shared together. Grandfather Rajah-Ganga Bugalaa, for that was his name, had committed many great acts of bravery during his long, earthly life. But one day he had

7

flown away into the sunset and never returned. Rumours had spread far and wide that he had finally dropped his physical body near the source of the River Ganges, at the Gaumukh Glacier, close to Gangotri and had been seen later by a wandering hermit appearing in exactly the same spot as a point of light, surrounded by rainbows for a full half hour afterwards and then had disappeared. But that is another story! Although the youngster had missed him greatly, he had a feeling that his beloved grandfather was not so very far away at all. In fact, it felt like he was continually being guided during his young life by his 'presence' close to him. He had also been named after his late grandfather and was known to all as Raji-B.

Raji-B and Saffron now had a permanent home together. Life became calm and acquired a certain regularity to it. People came and went past Saffron and they would sometimes pat her head or scratch her chin. She was a favourite in the neighbourhood and her owners loved and fed her well. They also came to accept the young bird who was always to be seen hanging around the place and who happened to have a very sweet singing voice. In fact, Raji-B soon became quite famous for his early morning and evening songs.

One day, they were sitting side by side quietly enjoying the warmth of the afternoon sun.

'You know what, Saffron?' said Raji-B as he helped himself to a little tic that had settled on young Saffron's neck, *'I would like to sing to you.'*

And so it was that Saffron shut her eyes and quietly listened to the sweet, dulcet tones of Raji-B. She felt contented. His voice carried courage and truthfulness and was so full of love.

Oh, how my heart yearns to merge with the Ocean,
That Ocean of Love I feel in my soul.

It is a call from my Centre that wants to be whole.
That Ocean of Love I feel in my soul.

Our love is an Ocean

An Ocean of love.

That Ocean of Love I feel in my soul.
When I sit beside you I feel I am whole.

Your heart is singing too,
I can feel it true,
That Ocean of Love I feel in my soul.

Our Love is an Ocean,
An Ocean of Love.

...And then he whistled a sweet flute-like melody which floated into the far beyond....

How Saffron loved that song. Raji-B had sung in his reed-like, purest, treble voice. It spoke to her of a longing in her deepest experience. She felt a surging within her heart. She could not quite define it but her mother had intimated such feelings.

Raji-B was intelligent. Saffron was in awe of his capacity to understand the meaning of life and of inner things; which could not be very well explained in any normal way.

      'What a gift he has,' she thought to herself.

      Whilst Saffron was thinking these kinds of thoughts, Raji-B mused about how this sweet young calf was an expression of the Divine Love that he felt inspired to sing about. To him, she was the world. Yes, these two were made for each other: such divine companions.

      What a blessed fortune that they had met. Umm ... he hummed on and he mused and he whistled quietly to himself ...

Our Love is an Ocean
An Ocean of Love.

The River Ganges, Ramnagar, Pashulok, Rishikesh

Chapter Three

High summer had come and Saffron was growing mature and strong, thanks to the love and generosity of her adoptive family. Raji-B was now fully grown in his radiant whiteness and had developed an elegant gait.

Saffron continually had tics and fleas jumping onto her coat and sometimes they jumped into her ears, which was most annoying. Raji-B instantly removed them. And whenever Saffron shifted from one spot to another, grasshoppers, flies or little mud worms would be his food. He never went hungry.

One day, Saffron and Raji-B were strolling near the Ganges. A dragon-fly flew by. He had the most beautiful rainbow-coloured wings that shone in the sunlight.

'How beautiful that creature is!' sighed Saffron.

'Yes, and without trying too,' said Raji-B.

'What do you mean by that?' asked Saffron.

'Well, we are all different aren't we? And we all have a beauty, unique to each one of us.'

'Yes, that is true,' said Saffron, *'you are a beautiful white bird and I am a brown cow. See how we get along together. How fortunate we are!'*

After a few moments, Raji-B glanced up at the clear blue sky and spoke:

'You know, when I first saw you, I knew you were a very special kind of cow. I was attracted to the energy that was around you. I do not know what it was exactly, but it just felt so special, so peaceful. I could not keep away, and now all my needs are cared for too. How fortunate I am.'

'Yes, I too am happy to know you, dear Raji-B. You have such a beautiful mind, so full of wisdom. Who taught you these things?'

'Well, you know that I had a very special grandfather and I loved him and totally trusted him. He taught me many things. He taught me how to go 'quiet' when things were troubling me and in that stillness I would find peace and answers to my problems. At first, I tried it and nothing seemed to work and I got despondent, but he continually encouraged me to keep trying. Then, one day something began to happen. It was a bit of a slow process, but soon I started to get in touch with that quietness. In the silence, I found that I became less agitated and more in control of my thoughts. It was remarkable. My grandfather really knew a thing or two! I have been practising it ever since.'

'Umm, how beautiful.' murmured Saffron. *'I had a wonderful and caring mother who also told me many things.'*

Chapter Four

A serene peace overcame the two of them as they meandered over to the river's edge and sat down with nose and beak very close to each other just by a small sandy bluff. Several rather splendid purple thistles grew nearby, their prickly leaves extending in all directions waiting to prickle anybody's legs who just might happen to be passing by. The river was making a gentle gurgling sound, and once more the little dragon-fly, whose wings shimmered rainbows, flew nearby enjoying the reflection-dance of the watery ripples as they trickled in the sunlight.

After some time, Saffron spoke:

'My mother seemed to have a sixth sense and she whispered many things in my ears, but I did not understand them very well at the time as I was too young. She was kind and had a good heart. Would you like to hear about them? I will tell you what blessings she gave me.'

There was a pause, then she said:

'She fed me on the milk of Compassion. She licked my face with the fragrance of the Beloved Divine One. She rubbed her shoulder on mine with the gentleness of remembrance and when I nestled into the warmth of her body, she instilled in me a sense of knowing in the un-knowing of my young life ... if you know what I mean.'

'Can you tell me more about this 'knowing?' asked Raji-B. *'Did your mother tell you anything more?'*

Saffron sat for a long while, quietly looking into the far distance. The sun was bright, and many birds were singing their beautiful songs of love, life and hope. She had a secret. It was a very special secret. Her dearest mother had indeed told her something about this *'knowing'* and now she really understood its meaning. She breathed very deeply several times and looked deeply into the eyes of Raji-B.

'Should she share it with him? Could he be trusted? Was the time right?'

They remained looking into each others' eyes for several minutes, then …

'Yes,' she thought, *this place is so peaceful. It is perfect and I feel he is very sincere. I can see that his heart is pure and I do so love him. I would love to share it with him.'*

And so it was that Saffron began to speak: to whisper the secret of her heart.

Chapter Five

Time stood still. It was as if nectar was dropping, drip by delicious drip, into Raji-B's thirsty and open heart. He had understood many things. He had learned so much from his beloved grandfather and yet … even as the leaves on the trees nearby, the blades of straggly grass, struggling for growth in this warm season, all shimmered in the sunlight, he knew. Yes, he KNEW without a doubt that there was *more* … this was what he had longed to know without really knowing what it was that he wanted to know.

The sky became a vast deep blue cavern suspended high over them. A pale, crescent moon floated on the ascendant. Little glistening dots of brilliant stardust sprinkled their fragrances of divine and secret light across that canopy. Slowly, everything turned into a luminous, liquid gold as the sun softly sent his radiant, shining rays of the early evening across this divine scene; pervading all things like an mantle over the flowing river.

'Mother whispered many things to me in her last days. I will share them all with you my dearest friend.'

A little tear trickled down her cheek as she remembered her mother's wise and powerful words. They were just *such* a beautiful memory for her. She was so very deeply moved by them.

'My darling child, you are the remembrance of all things: the clear blue sky above, the blessed, multi-coloured earth below.

When the winds blow, they are the loving caresses of the Divine.

When the mornings are misty or cold, remember that this is a call from Divine Grace to come closer to your heart to look and listen within to the many messages imprinted there.

Rains descend. The raindrops are the many blessings that give life and hope to all they fall upon.

When rainbows appear, especially in a black and cloudy sky, just remember that you

22

are being given a message of wisdom and courage.

The sun sends his warm, healing and sustaining rays downwards to bless and nourish even the smallest of created things.

The fragrances of the Divine are constantly being showered on all beings until a moment arrives when all are dissolved into that One Divinity. That moment is ever present and is known as Divine Grace.'

There was a long pause and then she continued.

'When you feel the wind on your face, the warmth in your bones, then know that at that very moment, you are being remembered by Divine Grace.

When you smell the perfume of a flower whispering past your nostrils, then know that at that very moment you are being blessed by Divine Grace.

When you feel the gentle touch of a human being, know that at that very moment you are being caressed by Divine Grace.

When you hear the sounds of any kind of music, whether it comes from anyone's voice, an instrument of any kind or just the breeze in the trees or grasses, know that at that very moment you are being spoken to by Divine Grace.

When you taste and eat the food that is offered to you, which has come from the Great Mother Earth Herself, know that at that very moment you are being nourished by Divine Grace.

When you have a positive thought in your mind and heart, know that at that very moment it is Divine Grace blessing your mind and heart.

When a negative thought enters your mind and heart, know that it is only a grey cloud passing across the Divine face of the sun up in the clear blue sky. It will not and cannot last.

Divine Grace is the very wind which will dissolve that cloud.

When you feel ill or hurt, or you feel lost and alone, know that at that very moment Divine Grace is bestowing on you the gift of courage and empathy, the gift of caring and loving others.

Because you have been given the very gift of life, know that you are of the substance of Divine Grace. You are never ever alone.

The secret is to remember that at all times and in all places, you are being greatly loved, protected and cared for both on the inside and the outside by Divine Grace every moment of every day that you live your life on this blessed Earth.'

Saffron became quiet. In the distance, the dulcet tones of a single reed flute floated on the gentle breeze of this beautiful Spring evening. It was a most heart-thrilling sound, ineffably divine and sublimely pure. The notes wavered and trilled as they danced and wove a magic in the air which transported all those nearby who heard it. Their hearts were open and tears rolled down Raji-B's cheek. Oh, how beautiful, how exquisite, how divine.

The flute played on and on as if caressing the very words that Saffron had spoken in Truth. The peace was inexorable, intoxicating.

Chapter six

Saffron took a long deep breath…

Her eyes were partially closed as she gazed across the sacred river towards the distant Sivalik hills. The feeling she was now experiencing was a total relaxation of her physical body. It was as if she could almost feel her devoted mother's warm body beside her, licking her ear. There was a calming, soothing sensation in her emotional state and her mind was oh, so peaceful; just like the clear blue sky above. She had the feeling that the Great Divine Mother was present right there and then, holding her in Her powerful and loving arms. A sublime moment.

Slowly, she turned her head towards Raji-B. The tears had ceased and his eyes were virtually closed as if he were focusing on something deep within himself. There was a long silence. Time stood still. Only the lazy buzzing of a nearby bumble bee could be heard as it busied itself around a rather large, exquisitely formed, purple thistle head.

The only way of telling how long this divine moment lasted was that the last shimmering, golden, red and orange rays of this beautiful and auspicious day had finally given way to deep indigo shadows which stretched across the valley. A very slight breeze whispered across Saffron's brow. The moon had risen and was riding high above the distant, silhouetted Himalayan foothills.

Silence stood still. Raji-B was profoundly moved. His mind totally acquiesced to this infinite moment. His little body almost quivering with extreme bliss as 'being-ness' flowed through him. He was speechless and thought free. Nothing disturbed his equilibrium. His eyes did not flutter. Darkness descended. He felt full of light. Yes, he felt that he *was* light.

Yet, still he sat.

Chapter Seven

Early the next morning, a small brown bird sat in rapture on a tree nearby, singing a delicate love song. The sweet nectar of the notes rising and falling just as the first rays of the sun fell across that heavenly landscape. No wind disturbed the trees. Still, Saffron and Raji-B sat side by side in close communion at the edge of the River Ganges. Beloved Mother Ganga was gurgling and rippling nearby. Her gentle laughter echoed around these twin souls who were now merged into the One Divine Consciousness.

'Divine Consciousness' was a wisdom that Saffron's mother had learned about from her own dear grandmother. She had had a profound experience of this Amazing Grace which had guided her own life according to that inner rhythm of Knowing. It was this valuable knowledge that Gaia had shared with her dearest child so that she might come to know and to understand before she died.

Now, Saffron really could feel her mother's presence sitting nearby ...

Yes, something had indeed happened. The lone mystic bird warbled on ...

The Night of ignorance has passed
The sun of a new day is born
You are the New Dawn

All shadows are dispelled
The sun of a new day is born
You are the New Dawn

Great news! Your hearts are open
Now awaken!
The sun of a new day is born
You are the New Dawn

The little bird continued her rapturous melody as the sun rose high into the sky. Three small, puffy white clouds gently floated by. An eagle soared majestically, circling high above on a current of air. A gentle breeze rustled the nearby sunburnt grasses and a dragonfly close to Saffron with rainbow gossamer wings flew by and sat on a rock.

A long, deep sigh was eventually heard from the direction of Raji-B. He blinked several times, and opened his eyes. Very slowly and gently, he stood up tall and stretched out his legs one at a time. He had lost the feeling in one leg because he had not moved for so long. He rocked gently to and fro on it to bring it back to life, then stretched each of his four toes out, flexing them one at a time until he could feel the energy flowing back into them. He scratched the back of his head and squinted all around him. A shining eagle was flying high in the sky. A dragonfly with beautiful sparkling wings was sitting so still on a nearby rock. The sun was suspended high in the sky. He noticed that his dearest friend was still seated silently beside him, but …

'Why, it must be mid-afternoon,' he mused to himself.

As he looked around, he noticed something extraordinary. Everything seemed to be shining in an unusual sort of way. He was shining. The rocks were shining. The beautiful River Ganges was glistening brightly as her flowing surface rippled this way and that. The trees were shining. Slowly, he turned his gaze again towards his beloved friend, Saffron. She was so shiny, he was dazzled and had to look away at first, until his eyes had re-adjusted themselves to the brilliance that surrounded her. She was sitting very still and so quiet, but her mouth was gently moving as she chewed the cud. To him, the world was at peace and at one with himself. He felt his consciousness had so expanded that there was no separation between him and anything else. The stones on the pathway, the people passing by, children's voices wafting on the air currents as they played in the distance: all was at One with itself and this included him. He felt so joyful. Nothing, nothing at all could disturb this moment. He felt free: free of disturbing and questioning thoughts. Wow! Whatever had happened to him, all his sadness had left his thoughts. He felt renewed and invigorated. The strange thing was, nothing had 'actually' changed. What *had* changed, he noticed, was his own view of everything around him. He felt *so* expanded. Now he saw and sensed things differently. He just 'knew'.

'So this is true 'knowing' ... he mused to himself. *'Umm.'*

Raji-B had been to the *far beyond* and returned. He felt different somehow. He was transformed. His mind was clear, without any doubt.

Now Saffron was standing up, shaking her head and stamping her feet. She bellowed so loudly that Raji-B almost jumped out of his feathers! Suddenly, she was racing alongside the river's edge and tossing her head up and down all at the same time. What a spectacle she made of herself! But she did not care. For a moment, there was a silence as everyone who happened to be around just then, stopped to stare. The dragonfly had long since flown away. The eagle had risen to different heights. The little brown singing bird had gone …

Raji-B shut his beak with a gob-smacked clack which made Saffron stop and stare at him. She felt great: wonderful, light. She could still feel her mother's presence beside her as she moved. She knew now that her mother would *always* be there beside her. Just because she did not have a body any more, didn't mean to say that she could not be present in another way. Yes, she was that very Consciousness that her mother had spoken of to her in her calfhood. In fact, Saffron herself felt so much part of the whole of the creation that she sensed a tremendous fullness: a love for all life and all beings.

She came and touched Raji-B's head with her nose and the two of them smiled at each other. They kept on smiling and smiling and smiling. Others around them looked across at them and wondered if they had gone mad. This was not normal behaviour for a cow and a bird, but we know better.

Saffron and Raji-B stood side by side staring out towards the sinking sun and bathing in its fading light before finally setting off back home, still beaming.

They returned with the Kiss of the Divine on their brows and hearts full of radiant joy.

The Call
of
The Divine

A Tale of Nine Birds

The Nine

Amritah (nectar). A young female egret. Quiet and shy. Her uncle is Raji-B, who appears in the "Kiss of the Divine".

Adinah (noble nature). Elderly male green parrot. A rough and ready sort but mild in his manner. Healer and expert in medicinal herbs.

Ajitah (unconquered), female and *Ananta (infinite),* male. Two young spotted doves in love with each other.

Ameya (boundless, magnanimous). A male crow in the prime of his life. Lisps. Is direct and purposeful when needed. Open and friendly.

Abhilasha (hope for great things). A female drongo in the prime of her life. Rather worldly.

Adesah (the teaching). Young male myna bird. Likes to sing and dance. Cheers others up.

Agnivalah (flaming as fire) A middle-aged, wreathed hornbill. Dignified, quiet, serious nature.

Alokah (transcending the worlds). Young female bulbul. Sensive and prone to visions. Sure of what she wants in her life.

Amarah (deathless) and *Anadi (eternal),* nightingales. Messengers for The Nine.

Chapter One

In the dim twilight of an Indian summer's evening, the lone, haunting song of a bird could be heard far away across the grey-green patchwork patterns of the shadowed meadows. The gentle breeze of a southerly wind lightly blew the leaves in the trees, making a soft, rustling sound. Stars were beginning to pop into evidence, twinkling brightly across the deep, turquoise sky in a haphazard pattern.

Each evening, as he had done for quite a number of years, a spritely and rather elderly singer would take it upon himself to welcome in the end of daylight and the beginning of night. His song was very welcome to those who could hear it. Tonight, however, he had something more important to share, thus his song was particularly clear and vibrant. Some of those who lived in the neighbourhood of Virbhadra, Rishikesh, an area of outstanding beauty and surrounded by the Sivalik Hills, were alert. There was something ... something one could not quite make out ... that seemed very persistent ... which struck a chord ... which resonated ... a knowing ... what was it?

Over the past few months, many rumours had been chirrupped abroad amongst the thousands of birds who lived in this neighbourhood. There had been a lot of chattering and twittering plus the usual general commotion created when news comes from afar. But no-one was more excited than a small number of birds who lived in a special tree and who were listening intensely, waiting for this moment. You may very well ask why they would be waiting for some seemingly insignificant event? We shall discover that in a little while.

These birds, along with their families and friends were a right motley crew who lived virtually on top of each other in a rather higgledy piggledy, oddly shaped, rough and tumble sort of tree that grew near a wide ditch on the edge of a large and stubbly field. The field was home to some young cows who were usually left to their own devices to wander around and graze where they could, on the sparse, straggly grass and weeds. Little white egrets followed them wherever they went, as food was easy to find in the form of tics, grasshoppers and little bugs disturbed by the cows' hooves as they grazed.

The 'Asvatthah' Tree
Virbhadra, Rishikesh,

Now, this special tree which was considered by some to have magical powers was home to these particular birds and was known locally as the Asvatthah tree of Virbhadra. A tale had been handed down the generations about a venerable old eagle who had become enlightened by sitting in the shade of its branches every day and muttering to himself *"ta-Gi, ta-Gi, ta-Gi"*. This was because an ancient Bengali sage had sat underneath the tree reading the *Bhagavad Gita** aloud and all the eagle could hear from his perch, was ta-Gi, ('Gita' with the spelling rearranged)! *'Ta-Gi'* actually means *'one who has renounced everything for God!'* In fact, the locals were led to believe that the eagle who was now resident in its upper branches was probably a descendant.

Eagle on 'Asvatthah' tree, Virbhadra, Rishikesh

He was a beautiful, rusty brown coloured eagle in the prime of his life, who lived with his wife in a large nest that was precipitously balanced between two branches. The couple spent a lot of time feeding their one and only, robust and voracious youngster. Father was also given to solitary reflection, perched on the uppermost branch of the tree. Underneath and to their left, lived a couple of crows. To their right and on the same level, lived seven or eight noisy parrots who spent all their time flying about in big, green swirls. Below and to their left, lived a rather aristocratic couple of wreathed hornbills who (actually) shared the same living quarters, surprisingly, as a family of rather non-descript, black myna birds who were also quite noisy and probably considered themselves as 'sitting tenants', ensconced in a very cosy nest deep in a hole half-way down the trunk of the tree. This tree split into three about a third of the way down and a pile of other interesting birds shared their home on another branch. Near the hole of the 'sitting tenants' and on the extreme left branch lived a young buzzard who had built a nest with his mate, obviously planning to start a family. They spent most of their time in competition for air space with the two eagles who lived above. Lower down, lived a solitary, black female drongo with her beautiful long split tail always neatly arranged. She was a lively character and talked a lot to herself whilst sitting alone on a long, single branch that hung out on its own over the ditch. One might have thought that she was lonesome, but she was not. In fact, she was very contented. Close by, on her right, lived a large family of bulbuls and in a bush further away were a couple of spotted doves who spent all their time courting each other, dancing and bobbing their heads up and down together and crooning to each other. They couldn't leave each other alone! Many other birds came and went with the passing of the seasons.

To outward appearances they seemed a pretty normal bunch of characters who got along well together most of the time, respecting each others' space and flying rights. The birds that stayed and settled in this tree were living proof that you don't have to be of the same kind or nature to live contentedly side by side. Indeed, amongst these birds there were a few unusually generous, kind and noble characters, as there often are in a successful community. They were the ones who had big hearts. They cared about each other and especially those who were young or weak. They were trustworthy and compassionate, generous with their listening time and sincere. Everyone in the neighbourhood loved and respected them. But then, this was no ordinary neighbourhood, situated as it was, close to an especially beautiful part of the River Ganges in Rishikesh, where many evolved souls lived.

The songster who had roused everyone with his enchanting melody was certainly no ordinary singing bird. He was a nightingale whose name was Amarah. It was rumoured that he had been an extremely brave and fearless bird in his time. And now he was calling out to anyone and everyone who would care to fly across the meadows to come and listen to what he had to say. Thousands of birds heard his divine song but only nine of them bothered to respond. Just nine birds, whose hearts were open and who had heard that special call, decided to go and listen to what Amarah had to say. They felt that that was the least they could do. They just *had* to go.

Many others had talked about going; had deliberated and debated at length. Some youngsters wanted to go for the excitement of a good flight out, especially at night time ... Their parents told them it was far too dangerous and would not let them go as they were too young and anyway, who was to say that it was not a trick? Could someone go and check it out, please? Well, nine had already left so no doubt someone, they presumed, would report back and tell them what it was all about and whether or not it was important. And so they stayed just where they were in the usual routine of their little lives.

If one looked and listened carefully enough, those nine birds could be seen and heard leaving their homes one by one from different parts of the tree. There would be a little rustle or two, here and there, then some sweet conversations could be heard as discussions and various goodbyes were taking place. Their exodus from the tree and nearby bushes was almost a simultaneous event as a flurry of wings and shadows could be seen rising up and heading out towards the direction of the lone singer.

Chapter Two

Away the birds flew from their homes in Virbhadra. They rose as if one body, higher and higher until they were far above the tree tops. Each one flying alone with his or her own thoughts about this extraordinary event calling to their hearts. They were met by a deep, night sky, lit by what seemed like a billion twinkling stars and a pale, shining, waxing moon.

As they travelled onwards, they tried to look across at each other to see who had come, but of course no one saw very clearly. They could only make out dim shapes. They flew on and on until the song of Amarah was getting louder and clearer. There was a great excitement in the air.

Eventually, these nine birds saw a dark, rough looking mound in the distance rising out of the earth. On the top was a fairly robust neem tree, and on the topmost twig sat Amarah. He was alone. He looked positively huge in the dark. But we know that actually he was not a very large bird.

One by one, the birds slowly descended to earth, landing on the top of the mound a few metres away from where Amarah sat. They were all feeling tired and were glad to stop, but all were exhilarated by the flight and the wonder of it. Each one's heart was beating fast.

They looked around to see who else had arrived. They were the only ones. Just nine of them. Indeed, as we now know, they were the only ones to show up at all on this auspicious evening.

'How strange, we are the only ones,' they each thought. They then began to find out who had come and why, and at the same time, introducing themselves to the nightingale, Amarah.

Chapter Three

Out of the gloom, a beautifully sleek, white bird emerged. It was one of the egrets from the field below the tree. Although she was generally a timid sort, she was brave enough to speak up first, her little voice piping a shy introduction.

'Hello, my name is Amritah.' There was a short pause as she caught her breath to ease the pounding of her heart. She continued, 'I have always loved the sound of that singing bird's voice whenever I've heard it. So, now I have come here because my uncle, whose name was Raji B, and some of you may have heard of him, said that one day a message would come especially for me from afar. He was not sure how, or by whom, but he said that I would definitely know it when it came. This time, it feels like this is it. That is why I am here. And ... oh yes, er ... I live in Virbhadra.' She then immediately turned towards Amarah, dropped her head in great humility and sat down.

Everyone murmured their greetings and showed their gratitude for her presence.

Amarah sat patiently and silently listening as each in turn came forward and introduced themselves to him and to one another.

There was a sudden rustle to one side and a rather dishevelled and elderly, male green parrot appeared and started to speak. His voice was a little rough and ready, but his tone and manner were gentle.

'I could not contain myself when I heard this message. How my heart missed a beat! It felt like a great opportunity for me and I just had to come. I am fairly elderly now and have always taken care of my family, but now there are others at home who can do that, which leaves me free to come and go. I come with their blessing. So, here I am. My name is Adinah and I live in Virbhadra in the Asvatthah tree. He moved away and sat down.

By now, everyone was feeling a little more brave, and slowly but surely, the group began to huddle closer together so they could hear each other more easily. Suddenly, there was a lot of fidgeting and pushing at the back of the group. Then the two young spotted doves, who lived in the bush near the rough and tumble Asvatthah tree, fluttered into view. The rest of the group were truly surprised to see these two coming out, as all they seemed to do was to bill-and-coo at each other and not think about anything or anyone else!

'Such a shallow pair!' some thought.

'Well,' thought several other birds, 'you just don't know what is really going on inside each one of us.'

The doves were laughing merrily together, their eyes shining bright. They were so overcome by their emotions that they could not speak for a moment or two. Everyone else remained quiet and expectant. Then they both began to speak at once and they started to laugh again. They always found themselves speaking the same thing at the same moment.

Finally, the smaller of the two spoke

out: 'Greetings, my name is Ajitah and my sweetheart here is called Ananta. There was a short pause then they became quite serious.

Ananta started to speak, 'Yes, we have come and we are both deeply in love with each other so could not leave the other one behind; we may seem young but we are very serious about wanting to understand the meaning of life, and this seemed like a great chance. We both wanted to come and here we are. We live in Virbhadra too, close to the Asvatthah tree.' This time, everyone started clapping and cheering.

'How lovely,' some thought.

'How sweet,' thought another.

'What a remarkable thing to do,' some others pondered. Quietly, the two love birds moved to the side and sat down almost on top of each other and they laughed again. The atmosphere was becoming electric.

Next, a crow waddled into the circle and announced himself. He had a bad lisp. 'Yeth, er – hello. I am Ameya. I have altho come from Virbhadra. I came becoth my friend wanted to come and she ith here with me now.' There was a pause and out of the shadows hopped a luscious black drongo with a little white beauty spot on her cheek and sporting a fine, silky black, long split tail which she splayed out behind her rather in the manner of a bride's train. 'Thith ith Abhilasha.'

'Greetings,' she said as she mimicked the lovebird, Ajitah, who gave her a strange sideways glance. Suddenly, the crow nudged her sharply and she staggered a little.

'Juth be yourthelf,' he said. 'You don't need to play your fanthy games here.' Everyone there immediately recognised her and all knew that she was an awful mimic. She often pretended to be someone other than she was, with the sole intention of stealing their food when they got distracted and weren't looking. She then continued in her normal voice.

'Okay, Ahem.' She cleared her throat as if she was about to make an important speech. Someone in the background muffled a giggle. 'I have led such a wasteful life till now. I am

55

thoroughly fed up and extremely bored with my present circumstances. I want a change.' She paused, then said, 'That is why I am here. I am not the empty-headed person that some of you may think me to be. My friend Amaya, will vouch for that, won't you dear?'

'Yeth, yeth indeed. She ith a very truthful and rethpectable lady now,' he cawed, at the same time flapping out his wings so that they ruffled Abhilasha's tail feathers.

'I am hoping that I might get some help here,' she ended.

The rest of the group started murmuring in a rather more positive way and Amarah also smiled in agreement. He had seen the truth in what she had said by the twinkling of her eyes. Without further ado, they both bowed very graciously towards him and merged back into the shadows.

If you could have seen the view from the perspective of Amarah's perch, you would have seen a lot of happy, smiling faces all around.

'Good gracious!' Everyone was agog. Great scrabblings, flappings and squeekings were heard from the back of the crowd. Just about everyone's head was completely screwed around to see who and what was causing such a hullabaloo. Out of the gloaming, appeared a very strange sight. No-one could quite make it out in the darkness. Then, three birds of different statures came fumbling forward, pushing and shoving each other to go first.

'No, no! Not me, not me!'

'You go first.'

'Hey, who do you think you are shoving? You are bigger than me!'

'Get your feathers off me!'

'Okay, okay I'll go, just ... just don't push!'

In hobbled three birds in order of size. The first to enter was a wreathed hornbill, next came a myna bird and thirdly a red whiskered bulbul. They took up their positions in front of

57

everyone. You could have cut the atmosphere with a knife. Not a sound was heard. Everyone recognised the myna bird and the wreathed hornbill as being part of the menagerie who shared the hole in the middle of the Asvatthah tree!

The myna bird started to speak, 'I am Adesah.' Then he surprised everyone by starting to dance. He stretched out his wings, picked up his feet one at a time and began to chuckle and click, chortle and whistle, singing a merry old tune. He flicked his tail feathers this way and that as he sang and danced. This performance carried on for quite a few minutes and everyone started to sway and bob in time with his melodic dance. This particular chap was very well known and was a great party-goer. He could entertain, amuse and joke about, making the most miserable of creatures begin to smile. Indeed, he was very talented. Then he stopped and stood waiting until all the noise had died down.

Adesah immediately introduced the other two birds. 'Here is my good friend Agnivalah and he pushed forward his friend, the wreathed hornbill.

He stood up straight, smoothed his feathers down and began to speak: 'Oh, how I have longed to meet the bird whose most recent call has brought me here tonight. It rings of the truth. I want to know more of this, thank you, thank you.'

He stood back and encouraged the small bulbul to step forwards and to introduce herself. This bird was very sweet and had a pointed, punkish looking topknot on her head and a longish tail. She didn't speak at first, but gently looked around her at the crowd of expectant faces. She seemed to look into their very souls as she surveyed each one there. She opened her beak and offered a most enchanting, long note. Then she began to speak. Her voice came over as strong and articulate.

'Greetings my friends! My name is Alokah. I have come from Virbhadra and I also live in the Asvatthah tree with these other friends. My heart prompted me to leave my family nest and to fly here, knowing that I would be amongst kindred spirits.' She looked around again and a tear trickled down her little feathery cheek. 'I, I once had a dream not so long ago of

59

a beautiful soul who sang me a similar song to that sung by Amarah here. He ... he,' she sniffed, 'and ... and ... he lived at the foot of a very sacred and beautiful mountain in the South. A very long way from here ... oh ... oh ... oh ...' She couldn't go on. She was moved by tremendous emotions and her chest heaved up and down in great convulsions. She continued, 'in this dream the melody spoke to me in my heart.'

Slowly, Alokah became calmer and stronger as she regained her composure. There was complete silence. Everybody was really interested in what she was saying. 'I have come because I feel that this is a great opportunity for me although I do not know the full impact of what it is yet'. She paused. 'Thank you all for listening to me.' She sat down right where she stood.

In great wonderment, a hushed silence had overcome them all and they sat still for quite a while, not saying a word. Everybody had had their say and each one began to feel a sweet contentment and peace descend upon them.

In that deep and pervasive silence, everyone relaxed and let go of any forebodings or misgivings they may have had about coming there. They were amongst friends now for sure.

Amarah began to speak: *'Welcome, welcome, and welcome again,'* he said. He shook his feathers, *'I am delighted to see you all here. I see that there are just nine of you. So few, but what a lovely lot you are. Thank you for coming. Now please do all go and refresh yourselves in the Ahi, which incidentally means 'Heaven and Earth conjoined,' which is just below us. Then we will meet again here.'* So saying, Amarah flew off his perch and swooped down towards the small stream. Everyone else followed on. Now, they felt they could go and drink and have a good bath from the little flowing stream which they had in fact all noticed when they had arrived earlier.

After a good drink and a great deal of splashing, ducking and diving, everyone felt refreshed and gradually made their way back up the hill towards the bushy tree that sat on the top. They were very tired by now and Amarah invited them all to take a good rest and to find a perch in the tree or wherever they felt comfortable. They would all meet again the next day at dawn. He would call them.

Each bird wished one another goodnight and disappeared into the darkness and undergrowth for a well-earned sleep. Silence fell. Crickets chirrupped. Soft rustlings could be heard in the surrounding grassy fields as little night creatures ventured out of their homes in search of food. An owl hooted in the distance and the night breezes gently blew across the landscape. All the birds were very soon sound asleep.

Chapter Four

Let us take a moment now, to look at all these dear characters who had so willingly flown into the unknown because they felt that there must be more to life than they could possibly fathom. They really wanted to *know*. They had felt a vibration, a quickening in their hearts that had called them away from the comfort of their perches to search for true meaning in their lives. What could they do? They just had to answer the call.

Amritah, the young egret came from a family who had lived in the Virbhadra area for many generations. Her uncle had been the great Raji B who had become fully realised right beside the River Ganges and whose story was still being told amongst the locals. She was intelligent and wise beyond her years and many of the youngsters looked up to her for guidance and direction. In all her dealings with others, she was loving and gracious. Her parents adored her and believed that she was destined for some great event that would transform her life.

Adinah was an elderly green parrot, who hailed from Mussoorie, a beautiful hill station in the foothills of the Himalayas. He and his wife along with their two youngsters had moved down to Rishikesh during the severe monsoon rains of the previous year. They were relative newcomers to the Virbhadra area, but had settled down quite happily in the Asvatthah tree and were tolerated more or less by the rest of the neighbourhood. Adinah was highly respected amongst his own kind for his deep wisdom and knowledge of medicinal herbs and plants. He was a healer who had helped many an injured or sick bird during the course of his long and varied life.

One day, during one of his excursions whilst looking for rare herbs, Adinah had come across a solitary *Wise One* who spent most of his days in meditation sitting beside a small stream not far from his cave deep in the mountains. Adinah had got into conversation with him and was very impressed by his wisdom and beautiful face, which was full of love. He had stayed for many hours sitting with this sage who eventually initiated him into the whispered lineage of the

Ancient Himalayan Masters. His initiation enabled him to help many others and sometimes he whispered secret formulae into the ears of mentally ill birds who then became totally healed in a matter of hours. He had also served as a member on the Great Council of Healers for several years and now he was too old to make the journeys for herbs any more. He wanted, more than ever, to retire from the world and live a life of prayer and solitude. His family had been against it for various reasons and so he had remained at home.

Ajitah was a beautiful young female spotted dove who came from a family of wanderers. They had never spent longer than a season in any particular area but now they felt like settling down, as the pickings were good and the neighbours were welcoming. There were a couple of humans living in a cottage nearby who fed them from time to time. She had recently met Ananta and they had fallen in love. They planned to have a family, but as soon as they had heard that magical call from afar, they had responded to it immediately, putting everything else on hold for the time being.

Ananta, a quiet type, was a great thinker. He had been raised in Virbhadra along with his two younger brothers. As a youngster, he had been very placid and easy going. His parents were gentle folk who lived quietly in their own way not far from the famous Virbhadra temple. He was a philosopher and was often seen chatting to the local sadhus or spiritual holy men. He had his own views on things, and always enjoyed a good discussion. In fact, that was how he met Ajitah. She had been sitting nearby, listening in on one of his conversations and was impressed with Ananta's deep wisdom and understanding. They had caught each other's eye during a lull in the conversation, and now they were living together in Virbhadra near the Asvatthah tree, with the blessings of both sets of parents.

Ameya was a black, shiny crow whose family had always lived in Virbhadra. He had a serious lisp and was a bit shy as a result, but was direct and purposeful whenever needed. Others liked him as soon as they met him because he was open-hearted and friendly. Ameya, a bachelor, had never shown any interest in having a family. He was in the prime of his life, full of bounce and always ready for a bit of excitement in whatever shape or form it would appear. So when 'the call' had come, which he and his friend Abhilasha had heard, both had wanted to go. He was keen and decided to accompany her to find out what it was all about.

Abhilasha, a neighbour and a good friend of Ameya, was a rather 'fancy' black drongo, who spent most of her time preening, washing, scratching and shaking her long tail. She spent hours picking at her wings and laying them smoothly on both sides to make herself look as sleek as possible. She was vain and an only child and had been close to her mother who had died a few weeks earlier. Her father had disappeared long ago. She was sad and lonely. Kind Ameya had helped her to do her grieving properly. Now she felt so much better and was happy to have such a good friend nearby.

Adesah was a rather cheeky, happy-go-lucky and bold myna bird. He came from a very large family who had lived for generations in the

Asvatthah tree. None of his family members had ever been interested in the spiritual side of life. In fact, Adesah was the first as far as anyone could remember, to show any sign of interest in anything other than worldly concerns. He had immediately responded to 'the call' along with his two close friends Agnivarah and Alokah.

Agnivalah, a middle-aged male wreathed hornbill who, along with his loving wife, shared the hole in the tree trunk with Adesah's family for such things as feeding, breeding and conversation. The wreathed hornbill couple had had no children and were not interested in having any either. They were socialites who enjoyed entertaining and being entertained just to pass the time. It was a wearysome life for Agnivalah who was beginning to tire of the eternal round of what he saw as meaningless activities. He had felt a 'stirring' of sorts in his heart which made him restless. He didn't fully understand quite why he felt so discontented. He just wasn't happy inside any more. His wife had been most disconcerted about him as his eyes seemed to have a permanent glaze of listlessness over them. So when 'the call' had come, she had encouraged him to go and find out what it was all about. Perhaps it would cheer him up. She was always very kind and he was most grateful to her for encouraging him to go.

Alokah, a pretty little bulbul, was quite young, but mature for her age. She looked upon Agnivalah as a kindly and loving father figure as she had lost both of her parents when she was very young and had been adopted by some concerned neighbours in the Asvatthah tree. Nobody knew what had become of them. Most of those who knew her thought she seemed a rather sad little thing, as she spent a lot of time on her own. Really, she was in contemplation. She liked the silence and it gave her a chance to clear her mind and just think. Alokah was a bit of a visionary and tended to live her life depending on what her inner voice told her. She had just been talking with Agnivalah when the beautiful melody of that distant songster had wafted across the valley towards them. At that very moment, Adesah had turned up wanting to respond to the call, so after saying their farewells to friends and family, the three of them had left immediately.

Chapter Five

The next morning, all the birds rose, refreshed and ready for the day ahead. Each one stretched his or her feathers out, then scrabbled off in search of bugs, tics, seeds and any other foods that they could find in the locality before the sun rose above the horizon. Then they all met down by the little stream. Amritah, the egret, was the first one there. She had already bathed and taken a cool drink by the time the others joined her.

What a jolly sight it was, seeing all the birds washing and drinking and generally causing a great commotion in that early dawn. There was a lot of twitterpating, splashing and clucking going on. Finally, they finished their toilet and flew about this way and that, drying themselves off before they flew up towards the neem tree. They were all friends now and had had a good chance to get to know each other. The dawn breeze was still cool, but the warming rays of the sun were beginning to glint orange and gold above the tree tops in the far distance ushering in the new day and creating shadows that danced out across the distant landscape.

'Oh what beauty it is to behold,' thought Amritah.

Amarah, who had had his bath much earlier on, sang his morning call and was waiting patiently on the topmost branch of the neem tree for all to arrive. The sun's rays crawled right up the hill to the top of the tree until his brow shone bright, making him look like a shining being straight from heaven.

Soon, The Nine, as they came to be known, arrived and sat near the tree. Each having found a comfortable branch on which to perch. Amritah the egret chose to sit near the base of the tree along with Ajitah and Ananta the love doves. They settled down to hear what their hearts had responded to, all turning their attention and eyes to that beautiful singer at the top of the tree who was bathed in pure sunlight. He looked magnificent. Silence fell.

Slowly, the sun came up above the

horizon and shone warmth on all at this blessed little gathering. The gentle breeze stopped completely as if it also wanted to hear every syllable that was being uttered.

Amarah began to speak, *"Oh my friends. Each one of you is most welcome here. I see that your hearts are on fire with love and friendship. Each one of you has been called. You have listened and responded. How I love you all."*

He then embarked on a glorious prelude to his message. It was well-known amongst a certain section of society who particularly loved poetry.

*Listen to the Exhortation of the Dawn!
Look to this Day!
For it is Life, the very Life of Life.
In its brief course lie all the
Verities and Realities of your Existence.
The Bliss of Growth,
The Glory of Action,
The Splendor of Beauty;
For Yesterday is but a Dream,

73

And To-morrow is only a Vision,
But To-day well lived makes
Every Yesterday a Dream of Happiness,
And every Tomorrow a Vision of Hope.
Look well therefore to this Day!
Such is the Salutation of the Dawn!

Each of The Nine sat enraptured:

'Oh, how divine,'

'Oh bliss, bliss, oh...'

'Ah, heavenly'.

'Yes, yes, yes!'

'It makes my heart sing.'

Every so often, these and similar utterances could be heard from the group. Not a few tears were also shed as hearts were awakened. What a divine company this was becoming! At the end of the song, silence descended and embraced each one where he or she sat. No sound could be heard for what seemed like an eternity.

Amarah sat for a long time in silence on his perch at the top of the tree patiently waiting for everyone to emerge from their reverie. Oh what a delightful scene it was. How it warmed his heart to see that, although numbers were few, these birds were possibly the hope for the future. He saw how each one had been deeply moved by his prelude. They were ready to hear what he now had to say to them.

He spoke out clearly and lovingly. It was as if he spoke to each one's heart directly:

My dearest friends, each one of you is being called upon, to fulfil your destiny and to make yet another journey. This time, to a sacred mountain in the South of India. My brother Anadi is living near the top of it and will lead you to your heart's desire. He is a great and generous soul. He will enable you all to understand the truth of your existence. He will offer you help so that you may become a source of strength to others who are very much in need of your skills in these difficult times.

The world is suffering from a great

sickness. The loving heart has been sidelined in the doings of beings who inhabit this planet. There is disharmony amongst the creatures, great and small. Wars are being fought because of misunderstandings and greed. There is no real love left. No-one really knows what true love is any more. Where is the loving heart? So many others are locked into the workings and connivings of their small minds. They have lost touch with their feelings. Their little selves have been caught up in the glossy materialism of their lives. The scheming mind has taken the place of the loving heart. We all know that the heart and the mind must work together in order to have balance and justice in society. When we see harmony and peace all around us, what is happening? Do we not see that it is the heart and the mind working together? The world is certainly in need of a remedy.

Now, when I speak of the mind, I am talking about our conscious, analysing, cognitive mind. I am speaking about our reasoning mind. The mind that says whether this is good or that is bad. The desiring bit of mind that says I want this and I don't want that. This kind of mind leads us to do or act in good or bad ways. This is the mind of our own selfish attachments and wishes. Is it not so, my friends, that we always have to look to the bigger picture? And that is where the heart comes in.

Of course, we need our minds to guide our hearts, but we also need our hearts to temper our minds with love and compassion. We are all part of the great divine plan. No one is exempt, however small and insignificant we may feel. Every single one of us is interconnected through the invisible 'mantle of eternity' and therefore we must understand that, - because of our inter-connectedness, what we do for others we are actually doing for ourselves. If we love or hurt another being then we are surely loving or hurting ourselves. Very few really understand this eternal law.

Let me tell you a story about us being interconnected:
'Once upon a time, there was a small spider. He was intelligent and inquisitive. He used to sit

still in a corner of his web in the very early mornings waiting for the sun to rise and then he would begin to contemplate the meaning of life. This was the best part of his day as he loved the sun and its attendant warmth.

One day, as he was sitting quietly with the sun just beginning to send bright, warming rays across his back, he noticed something he had never seen before. He could not believe his eyes. As he looked out over his web, he noticed that there were many dew drops spread out right across it, although this, in itself, was nothing new. Many times he had seen the dew drops resting on his web, but now, he really saw something amazing. He looked and looked, and he saw that each dew drop was shining bright, reflecting the morning sun, but on looking closer, he noticed that when he focused particularly on one dew drop, he could see the reflections of all the others just in that single one.

'Wow!' he thought to himself. 'That is truly amazing.' 'Now,' he carried on thinking, 'What if I were to make my web, complete with all its

multitude of dew drops resting on the surface, extend in all directions for ever and ever, so that an infinite reflecting process was occurring all the time? What would happen?'

'Ummm, let me see ... I would discover that I am an integral part of this universe. How amazing! Now, if I was to consider myself as being one of these dew drops, and all other beings in the whole wide world as also being a dew drop, whatever I do, say, or think, and whatever everyone else did, said or thought, would be reflected in all other dew drops, ad infinitum. Wow! That is scary. No wonder we are in such a mess in the world. And no wonder troubles keep coming my way. But nice things also come my way too...ummmmm.' He carried on thinking. Then something else occurred to him. 'Not only that, but I could also be eternal. Am I eternal? If we are all seen as just "one" happening in the myriad dew drops, then we all must be eternally "one" ...' He carried on thinking in this way. Then he thought: 'If I am eternal, and all other beings are also eternal then we are all one ... ummm. Wow!'

Everyone was silent. Each one in his or her own way had understood this story. It was very powerful. Not a word was spoken until they all flapped their wings and stamped their feet in acknowledgment.

'Yes, yes, yes,'

'What a good story,' and other such comments could be heard being expressed amongst the birds.

Then, when the noise had died down, Amarah continued: *You have all come, responding to my song, but truly, you were responding to the call of your own inner heart's yearning. You all love and have been loved. You have been touched by the Hand of God and you are the ones who have been chosen for this special task. I will tell more, but for now please go and take food, bathe and rest. We shall meet after that.* Then he flew away.

Chapter Six

Amarah was gone in a flash, leaving the others bewildered and open-beaked. Everyone watched him go. Each bird lost in his and her own thoughts.

'That story was amazing!'

'Wow! I am speechless.'

'If we could see like that.'

'Another journey?'

'Oh, it's such a long way to fly all the way down to the South.'

'Can we do it?'

'We shall be away for such a long time...'

'Who is this Anadi?'

'At least I am not having to go alone.'

'Oh, goodness me.'

'I am scared.'

'We must have courage.'

'We have been chosen, so, maybe, we shall be okay.'

'Oh, I shall miss my family and friends.'

'Will they forget me?'

These and many other mixed up thoughts occupied their minds but there was one bird who was thinking along quite a different train of thought. Alokah, the bulbul, moved slightly away from the others. She sat very still and stared into the far distance. She watched the clear, straight flight path of several migrating birds high up in the blue, cloudless sky, on the wing.

'Umm ... I wonder where those birds are going...?' she thought to herself. Then the memory of a beautiful dream that she had had some time ago wafted across her mind. She had dreamt of a bird who had sung a divine song to her and who lived on a hill in South India. The longer she focused on this thought, the more excited she grew.

'Is this a dream or a premonition? Could this really be happening to me?' She started to weep a little as the dream became clearer and clearer in her mind's eye. At the same time, waves of beautiful feelings of the dream re-manifested themselves, totally enveloping her little being.

'Oh, oh, I am so nervous – yet, at the same time, I am excited. I can hardly contain myself.' The tears eventually dried up around her eyes and she began to smile inwardly: a warm, glowing, heart-warming smile, until the feelings all came spilling out and her little face was beaming all over.

Alokah glanced across towards the others but they had all dispersed. She had been so engrossed in her own thoughts that she hadn't noticed any other movement around her. She decided to fly down to the little stream that Amarah had mysteriously called the Ahi, to have a drink. She thought about that name – the Ahi. Amarah had said that it meant 'Heaven and Earth conjoined'. She wondered what he had meant by that and decided that she would ask *Amarah* more about it the next time she saw him.

Whilst she was busily thinking about the Ahi, the two spotted doves, Ananta and Ajitah approached her.

'Oh, hello,' they cooed, 'hope we haven't disturbed you?'

'No, no, not at all,' said Alokah, looking up and smiling.

'You are the one who mentioned having had a dream about a singing bird and a sacred mountain far away from here, during the first introductions aren't you?' said Ananta.

'Yes, that's right.'

'Can you speak more about it?' asked Ajitah.

Gently, Alokah looked at them both. 'How beautiful they are in their spotty coats and so youthful,' she thought quietly to herself. 'Why, they must be younger than me.'

Then she said, 'I am deeply moved about all that is happening here. I don't quite know what to say. I ... I,' she whispered, 'er ... had this dream. Yes, it is amazing. It is so synchronistic that Amarah should mention it too and the fact that we have to make a journey to the South.' There was a pause. Then she got her courage up and said, 'Actually, I am very excited about it. It must be true. My dream is very important. Certainly for me and perhaps for all of you too. Who knows? All I know is that this Holy Hill, whatever it is called, is a very sacred spot and many pilgrims go there. The message I heard in my dream was so beautiful, I can't begin to tell you. But it is enough to make one's feathers stand on end and to send one into ecstasy.'

At that moment, Agnivalah, the wreathed hornbill, swooped down and sat beside Alokah. They both rubbed their cheeks together. One could see that they were truly fond of each other and such good friends. Alokah could share her innermost secrets with Agnivalah and he would never betray her. He loved her as a daughter and she loved him as a father.

The doves cooed their thanks and immediately flew off in search of food, leaving Agnivalah and Alokah alone.

'How are you feeling my dearest child?' asked Agnivalah.

'I am so amazed that Amarah mentioned the Hill in South India. As you know, my special dream was about the very same place.'

'Yes,' he replied. 'You are indeed very blessed.' He paused, 'have you eaten yet, dearest?'

'Not yet, but I will go now,' she said.

'Do you know where the others are?'

'I think everyone has gone off in search of food. I am pretty hungry myself, so I will see you later.'

'Thank you so much for caring about me,' she said. 'I love you so much and I am so happy that you are here. You give me courage.'

Quietly, she sat alone in the stillness with a beautiful feeling of warmth and love for Agnivalah who had looked after her since her childhood.

Chapter Seven

Later that afternoon, in the shade of the neem tree, several huddles of birds could be seen having intense discussions. Amritah, the egret, was speaking to Abhilasha, the drongo.

'You know, I think that this could be the message that my uncle Raji B once told me to expect some day. I feel it in my bones. Oh, I am so excited. Oh Abhilasha, I can hardly contain myself.'

Abhilasha smiled a little and said, 'I am truly pleased for you. It could be true. You seem such a good sort of bird, and kind too.' Then she said, 'Perhaps I can share something with you?' Amritah could sense that Abhilasha was wanting to open her heart.

'What can I say that would help her?' she thought to herself and offered her wing to Abhilasha as they sat in silence side by side.

Then she spoke: 'You know, I have to admit that I am feeling rather nervous about it all. I am not really sure what I think yet ... so much has happened, and you must agree that it is an awful long way to go. What will happen if we don't make it? I guess that I am feeling very afraid. But I do *really* want a change in my life. I know that I have led a rather selfish existence ... always thinking about myself, how I look, what I eat, who I mix with. You know, those sorts of things. Now I realise that I am always looking for distractions to fill my empty heart. My friend Ameya has always believed in me and probably knows me better than I know myself ... but I am so unsure. I probably give everybody the impression that I am an independent sort and that I don't need anybody else's help in anything.' Then she started to weep, 'Oh, oh, oh, she sobbed, but she did not and could not speak, her body was all a-quiver. In fact, she did not say any more, but cried on and on until Amritah thought she would never stop.

Meanwhile, just across the way, Ajitah, Ananta and Ameya were deep in conversation: 'Oh, I with I felt more brave than I do,' lisped

Ameya. Now, if Abhilasha could have heard her friend say that, she would have been totally shocked, for she had always thought of her crow friend as being stout-hearted and completely fearless. But right then, Abhilasha was otherwise engaged.

Ajitah and Ananta both began to speak at the same moment and laughed, quietly smiling at each other. Ananta spoke, having caught his breath and then he became serious.

'What are you afraid of, dear Ameya?'

'Umm, I thuppose I have alwayth put up a front of being thtrong for otherth. In my head I am very thtrong but in my heart I feel unthaw. What to do?'

Ananta spoke again: 'What is it you feel unsure about?'

'I think I do always feel thtronger when otherth need me. If they need thom help, then it ith eathier for me.'

'You know,' interrupted Ajitah, 'you

91

will be just fine with all the rest of us around you, supporting and encouraging you. We will all need your friendship and warm nature too.'

Adinah could be seen in all his green splendour discussing something vehemently with Adesah and Agnivalah whilst little Alokah sat listening to them on one side.

He was saying to Adesah, 'But, but, but...I am elderly and I am wondering whether I'll be able to make the journey all the way there.'

'Of course you will. If you have a strong wish to go, then you will be able to make it,' countered Adesah, 'and we are all going to make the trip together. We shall look out for each other, won't we, Agnivalah?'

'We most certainly will,' the hornbill said, 'and if we are truly meant to go, then, in my humble opinion, we shall all make it!'

'Yes, yes, we will, we will!' repeated Adesah. The myna bird gave a little whistle and bounced around. He then said, 'We shall cheer each other up. We can tell each other stories. We will love and care for each other. We shall look out for each other. We must help each other. Indeed, we must.' Then he added, 'Your healing skills will be very useful to us all along the way too.'

All this time, the little bulbul had said nothing but suddenly, Alokah spoke up and changing the subject, said, 'My goodness me, the time has passed by so quickly and the sun is high. It must be quite late. Do you think we should go and see if Amarah has returned?'

'Oh, that is a good idea' they agreed.

'It is really late. I wonder where the others are?'

'Yes, we had better go quickly. We don't want to be left behind, do we?' So up they flew to the top of the hill where Amarah had just returned to his topmost branch. He was silently looking far into the distance.

The others must have thought similar

thoughts wherever they were, as by this time all were swiftly making their way back up the hill to attend the gathering of The Nine. It had been Agnivalah who had called the group 'The Nine'. He had said it was a title that was strengthening and uniting and it suited them. They had all agreed.

Chapter Eight

By now, Abhilasha was a little calmer. Everyone stopped their chatterings and soon all were settled down on grass or branch ready to listen to Amarah who gently began to sing. He sang quietly at first then built it up to a crescendo:

*This is love:
To fly to heaven,
Every moment to rend a hundred veils;
At first instance,
To break away from breath –
First step, to renounce feet;
To disregard this world,
To see only that
Which you yourself have seen.

Amarah's song could be clearly heard by all. It was sung so beautifully, several were moved to tears. Why, this songster had a real talent. He could move one to laughter or to tears in an instant and he could tell a good story too.

Greetings, my beloved friends. I hope you are well rested and ready. These are to be my last words, then I shall be gone. If you have any questions please do ask them at the end of what I am just about to share with you.

You are known as The Nine. That is a very special number because it is considered a sign of perfection and unity. Power exists through unity. You must travel together. You must be loyal to each other. The unity of you all will bring many benefits. You must listen to each other, care for each other as much as you would care for your own welfare and well-being. This can be achieved through taking the time frequently to have a consultation together. Consultation is very important for your protection. Listen to me very carefully. These are the rules of a fair consultation. When making plans, you must discuss them all together and listen with compassion. Each of you must make it your duty to participate in every consultation that you have. If decisions are not obeyed, be aware of the consequences. It may work out or it may not. If a decision is carried out wholeheartedly by all of you, it will soon become apparent if the decision is a wrong one and it can be quickly reversed. Of course, if the decision is a right one, the benefits will be felt immediately by everybody. Ideally, you must endeavour to arrive at a unanimous decision and if this is not possible, then you must all take a vote and be guided by the majority. This is most important. Consultation is not truly about unity of opinion, although that helps. It calls for unity of purpose. I am sharing this with you because if you truly consult together, you will share peace, happiness and friendship so sweet.

Amarah shut his eyes and sang:

**The shining spark of truth cometh forth
only after the clash of
differing opinions.
Take ye counsel together in all matters,
inasmuch as consultation
is the lamp of guidance
which leadeth the way,
and is the bestower of understanding.
It is a shining light
which, in a dark world,
leadeth the way and guideth.*

Everybody was quiet. This was very powerful stuff. All were wondering what else he would say. A long time passed. The sun was high in the sky and the air was warm and still. Nobody moved a muscle.

It was late afternoon by the time Amarah spoke again: *My beloved friends. You must now all meet together in love and accord. Consult together. Decide together when you should leave this place and begin your journey. You know why you came here. You know what your heart is calling you to do. You will be fulfilling your destinies. You will become a source of great light and wisdom to all whom you meet once you reach your destination. This journey is truly to the destination of the heart. May the Divine Source bless you all. May your hearts be strong. Be determined, be single-pointed to achieve your goal. Above all, love and cherish one another. My good friend, Anadi will be there to welcome you all. You will be shown the way to find him once you get to the Holy Hill. He is waiting for you.*

There was a long silence.

Are there any questions?

Alokah immediately thought of the question that she had wanted to ask if she ever got the chance. She cleared her throat.

'Please excuse me. Yes, I have two questions to ask you. The first one is about the little stream below us, the Ahi. I was er ... just wondering if it had any special meaning apart from what you told us - that Ahi meant Heaven and Earth conjoined? Is it a special place? You see, where we come from, our home tree is called the Asvattah Tree which represents Heaven and Earth. And is that why we are the only ones who've heard your call?'

Amarah smiled and said, *Yes, that is so. The whole area here is also considered special. Over the centuries, this mound was revered by many great Oracles who gave out warnings and premonitions of future events. Many wisdoms were taught here. As you can now see, this hill meets the sky directly. If you like, the sky could be considered Heaven and the hill, Earth. One compliments the other. The stream just below us is the place of refreshment and renewal. It soothes the body and the soul with its continual flow. If you sit long enough beside the stream, it will tell you many things. Your tree has grown on sacred soil. Indeed, you have all been chosen. It is not by accident.*

'Thank you,' said Alokah. 'The other question I wish to ask is this. Whom should we appoint as our guide?'

Amarah said, *'You must consult together to find out who it shall be.'*

'Yes, please sir, I have a question,' piped up Adesah the myna, as he did a little hop at the same time. 'I would like to know what will be the most important thing that we must keep in our minds as we fly?'

Amarah looked intently at Adesah for a long moment, as if to 'feel' the impulse in his heart. Adesah felt a light current flow from Amarah's eyes into his, which touched his inner heart. It made him almost choke with emotion.

Love is the key. Love, love and more love. Think it, express it, show it and give it your attention at all times and in all places. Give it willingly to all whom you may meet along the way especially to those who will surely test you and cause you pain.

All were quiet. There seemed to be no more questions. Then Amarah spoke one last time.

Now, go. Bless you all. He sang a sweet song and instantly disappeared from view in a golden ball of light. Gone.

**In all situations maintain
a steady consciousness of Divinity
within and about you.
Do not harass your mind with
thoughts of weakness.
Infinite strength is within you.
Drawing inspiration and power
from this source,
be cheerful and contented at all times.*

Chapter Nine

For a long time, the fellowship of the Nine did not move. It was beginning to get dark and a cool breeze gently ruffled their feathers. A new moon floated silently into view. Here and there, little rustlings could be heard in the undergrowth as night creatures ventured forth to forage. An owl hooted in the far, forested distance which woke Agnivalah from his reverie.

'Oh, ah,' he stumbled and looked around at the others. Everybody was still staring at the void at the top of the tree where Amarah had just been.

Various comments could be heard like,

'Did you see that?

'He disappeared - just like that!'

'Wow! Now what do we do?'

'Oh no, we are all alone. What next?'

By now, the evening was drawing in and the company were tired and hungry. They also felt very alone.

'It's getting very late,' whispered Adesah.

Adinah, the parrot spoke up: 'We must talk. We must consult together.'

'Yeth, we mutht, we mutht,' echoed Ameya. Everyone drew closer together under the tree.

Then Alokah said, 'Dear friends, Amarah is gone. We are on our own now and we have to make some decisions, don't we? How does everyone feel if we first go and find some food, then we can sleep on what has been shared with us? It will take time for us to absorb all that has been said. Let's meet tomorrow at dawn and decide what to do next. We shall feel a lot fresher then and more clear-headed to make some decisions. What do you think?'

They all nodded but nobody else said anything, except Abhilasha, who was still with

Amritah. She had calmed down considerably and now she spoke.

'I am very impressed with what Amarah has shared with us. He has cheered me up no end. I am inspired. Yes, I think it is a great idea to rest now. Where shall we meet tomorrow?' Alokah suggested meeting at the Ahi after they had all eaten and bathed. Everyone agreed. Then silently they dispersed for the night.

'Good night.'

'Sleep well.'

'Tomorrow is a big day for all of us.'

'Yes, yes.'

'Good night.' Then Alokah added, 'Don't be afraid my friends. We are all in this together. Amarah really did believe in us, don't you think? Sweet dreams everybody.'

Chapter Ten

Early the next morning, after finding food wherever they could, the sounds of splashing and twittering could be heard drifting across the valley. It was still quite dark and little shadows could be seen moving about in the gloaming. Snatches of conversation could occasionally be heard. Eventually, a rather damp and bedraggled looking little group emerged to dry out on the bank of the Ahi.

Ameya was the first to speak: 'Now we mutht make a few dethithonth, muthn't we?' I wath very inprethed with what Amarah shared with us all, ethpethially about conthultation.'

Abhilasha was looking a little red-eyed from not having slept much, but she said, 'Yes, I was impressed too and I thought it was a very fair way to share our thoughts. It is important that we really do listen to each other. But first of all, we need a leader.'

'I have an idea,' said Ananta. 'What if we all took it in turns to be the leader, then everybody would have an opportunity to feel that they were being useful?'

'Why,' said Adesah, 'that's a good idea and we can make decisions as we go along. That is good consultation, isn't it?'

There was quite a heated discussion though about who should be the first leader. The problem was, that no-one really wanted to be first.

'Well, we have got to make a decision because we cannot stay sitting here for ever,' said Adinah. 'I have an idea. May I suggest that we all go and find a leaf, put it into a hole in the centre of our circle here, then the one who picks the biggest, must be our first leader. Of course, everyone must have their eyes closed when they go to choose their leaf out of the hole.'

'What a great idea,' they all agreed. Agnivalah volunteered to dig the hole as he had a big, strong beak. Everyone else flew off to find a leaf whilst Agnivalah looked around for a suitable place and scrabbled out a small but deep hole in the earth. Then he flew off to find his leaf. Soon they were all back, each having placed their leaf carefully in the hole, they then proceeded to sit in a circle around it. Amritah had the bright idea that everyone should go in turn, mix and poke the leaves before picking one and in that way they would all be well mixed up.

And so it was that each of these good birds in turn closed his or her eyes and picked out a leaf from the hole, then placed it in front of them. There was silence whilst they looked around at each other's leaf, impatient to find out who had picked the largest one. A small gasp was uttered as Amritah saw that she had the largest leaf right in front of her.

'Oh my,' she said. 'Oh no,' I can't be the leader.'

'Yes you can,' immediately cooed Ananta.

Ajitah agreed. 'We shall all help you, won't we?' she said as she looked around the circle. At that, everyone nodded in agreement whilst making encouraging noises that they would all try to be as co-operative as possible.

'All right, I shall do my best to be your leader,' said Amritah. She was still thinking about a message that she had received during the night. 'I don't know about you, but I didn't sleep very well. My uncle Raji B came to me again in my sleep. He said how happy he was that I was going on this trip and that I would meet someone on the way who will be very important for me. I was surprised to see him standing there. He seemed so life-like. You know, he died quite a long time ago.'

'I remember you telling me that,' said Abhilasha, 'you are obviously meant to be on this trip with us all, aren't you? I am on your side and I think you will make a good leader.'

'Thank you, dear Abhilasha,' said Amritah.

Then everyone started to speak at once saying that they too had experienced strange things in their sleep during the night.

Ajitah and Ananta spoke up in turn, 'Yes, we both had a dream. We even experienced the same dream,' said Ajitah.

'It was so amazing,' said Ananta 'that we should have the same dream simultaneously.'

'Yes, yes. Well let's hear it then,' said Adesah a little impatiently.

'Shhhh,' someone else whispered.

Ajitah spoke. 'In the dream we saw a huge mountain rising out from the plain and on the right side of it was a small tree which hid a cave. We heard someone speaking to us, though we could not see who it was. The voice said that we two are very special and that we are the embodiment of Love. We must play our part and become true Lovers. Then he sang such a sweet song to us:

I am the Mystic Lover
I call to your honey-filled heart

111

May you become intoxicated
May you play your part.

'How beautiful,' said Amritah. 'I
wonder who it was who spoke to you? You two
are most fortunate. I do sincerely believe that
you dear lovebirds, *will* play your part and will
each be a great force for showing us all how to
love and care for each other.'

Two spotted doves - Amrita and Ananta, Virbhadra

Chapter Eleven

Amritah was the leader now and she was taking her responsibility very seriously, making sure everyone would have their say and that all would endeavour to listen to each other.

'All of you, please do share what you wish,' said Amritah, 'for now is the time to open our hearts to each other and to say what is on our minds.'

Alokah then spoke up, 'Thank you dear Amritah. First of all, I am very happy that you are to be our leader. I will try to be of help to you if you should need it. Last night, I had a vision. At least, I think it was a vision. It seemed so real it feels like it is still with me. If I dared to shut my eyes, I would behold her beauty again and again. Oh ... yes.... A beautiful and luminous soul in rainbow radiance stood shimmering in front of me. She touched my head ever so softly with what seemed to be a long beam of light, and a great shock-wave went through my body.

Immediately I was transformed into light. At that moment, I felt connected to all things: the trees, the earth, the sky, everything. Just as if it were a part of me. Indeed, it felt as if it had always been like that, only I had never noticed before. All that I could see was bathed in this light and I felt a deep love in my heart expanding as I saw that we were all connected by a golden thread. I do not really know what it means but I have a strong feeling that we shall be looked after by a great loving force that is beyond our comprehension on the journey we are about to make. I feel so much love for you all too and privileged to be in your company.'

'Thank you dear Alokah. You are so wise and kind,' said Amritah. 'I think that we shall all benefit enormously from your loving support. Now who would like to speak next?'

Adinah hopped into the circle and began to speak, 'Thank you Amritah. You have my allegiance and I offer my services to the whole group. We are in this together. I am old and hope that I won't slow you all down on the way. I must tell you something. I also had a dream of an old friend who came to me in my sleep. He was that very same *Wise One* who had initiated me years ago into the tradition of the Ancient Himalayan Masters. In the dream, he picked me up ever so lovingly and held me in the palm of his hand and spoke soft words into my ear. I cannot recall them now, but I know that if I have a need, they will come to me. In fact, that is what he said. I feel that the *Wise One* will help to guide us all the way.'

'Thank you dear brother, Adinah. You are indeed blessed to have such a mentor. We will all benefit from your wise counsel and of course, your herbal and healing skills.'

Adesah spoke, 'If I can cheer everyone up along the way with my songs and stories, then I hope I will have done my bit. I shall trust you Amritah to guide us safely for this first bit of the journey. You have my full support. Thank you. Now, I did not have any visions or dreams of any sort, but I slept as soundly as a little chick all night long! I am ready to start this journey as soon as we can.'

'Thank you dear Adesah. I am pleased that you slept so well. Perhaps you will be able to keep a sharp look-out for us all. We will welcome your jokes and laughter too, won't we?'

Everyone agreed with a loud 'Here, here.'

Abhilasha spoke next, 'I could not sleep at all last night. It feels as if I only slept for a couple of minutes and I am feeling very tired. I couldn't sleep due to my mind chattering all the time so I went for a walk beside the Ahi. I came across another drongo relative and we had a little chat. Not about anything much though, but she did take my mind off things a bit with some girlie talk and laughs and ... oh yes... dear Amritah, I love you. You helped me so much yesterday when I was having a bit of a hard time. You have my full support, bless you. Oh ... and please can I have some time to take a cat-nap before we leave? - Oops, sorry, I hope I haven't offended anyone here. It's one of my silly expressions. I only mean a short nap! I am still so tired.'

'My dearest, of course, you must take a nap as soon as this consultation is over. Thank you for your support,' said Amritah.

'Fancy using *that* word,' muttered Adesah. 'I don't even make jokes about cats.' The others chose to ignore his comment.

Then Ameya spoke up: 'Oh,' he said. 'Oh ... oh ... umm.' He could not speak and only short utterences came out of his beak.

Everyone was silent, waiting to hear what he had to say. After a few moments more, he spoke, 'I dreamed that I wath thurrounded by many Divine Beingth. I feel thow nithe and warm, even now. I feel very thupported and ready for thith trip. Oh, er, um, I althow thlept very well. I mowht definitely thupport you ath our leader, Amritah. If I can be of help in any way I will do my betht.'

'Bless you, dear Ameya. Thank you so much for your generosity of heart.'

The last to speak to the group was Agnivalah. He had seemed a little downcast and quiet all the way through the consultation.

'I have had a very strange night. I slept well at first but then woke up in the middle of the night and thereafter only got small snatches of sporadic sleep. During this, I had an upsetting, albeit interesting dream. I dreamt that my wife had suddenly been taken sick from eating some poisonous substance and that she had died very quickly at the foot of the Asvattaha tree. The strange thing is that I seemed to be able to *see* exactly what was happening at the same time. The next thing I knew, she was sitting right beside me! Oh, I could feel the warmth of her body as she spoke, saying how much she was missing me and how much she loved me. She then said that she wanted to join us on this journey. I asked her what she meant by that and she said that now she was free to come and go as she wished and nobody at home would miss her. Then she said something about being be back shortly, and immediately disappeared before I could respond. I am trying to work out what it all means.'

'Dear, dear Agnivalah. I am so sorry but it does seem that your beloved wife may have left her body,' said Amritah. 'It sounds like she loved you very much. Perhaps she will soon re-appear?'

'Thank you.' He could say no more and Ameya instantly moved across and sat beside Agnivalah, stretching out his wing towards him. Neither spoke.

After a while Amritah spoke, 'Dearest brothers and sisters, thank you all for sharing your thoughts. I feel that we are becoming a close and loving group. Now, we have to decide what to do next. We must start our journey very soon.'

Chapter Twelve

'Is there anything that anyone wishes to talk about before we plan the journey?' As no-one had anything more to say, Amritah added 'Then please do take rest. Now is your chance to sleep, Abilasha.'

'Thank you,' she said and shuffled off to sit quietly on a branch.

'We now need a couple of you to help in planning the first bit of the journey, said Amritah. 'Is there anyone here who is good at sign reading?'

'Yes I am,' said Adinah.

'Good,' said Amritah 'and if anyone else wishes to join us for this discussion on sign reading, you are most welcome.' Both Ameya and Agnivalah immediately wanted to be in on the discussion.

'I am good at drawing, and I have been

shown by my friends what thith land thort of lookth like,' said Ameya.

'That could be very useful for we will need to know the best way to go,' said Amritah.

'I know a little about roads and trains,' enjoined Adinah, 'for that was the way some friends showed me when my wife and our family first came down to Virbadhra from Mussoorie.'

'Excellent,' mumbled a voice from the distance. It was Adesah just returning from a quick forage with a beak full of food. 'Can I join the discussion?'

'Good. Yes, yes, of course you can,' said everyone else.

Amritah, Agnivalah, Ameya, Adinah and Adesah slowly made their way to a shady corner under the neem tree.

Agnivalah was the first to speak, 'Do you remember Amarah saying that we should always try to meet together in love and harmony

122

or something like that?' The others nodded.

'Maybe it would be nice to have a little moment of silence before we begin?' suggested Amritah.

Agnivalah agreed, 'Yes, let's. What a grand idea!'

'What if we were to try and sing that song that Ananta and Ajitah had dreamt about. I really liked it,' said Adinah. 'Can we remember it? It was so beautiful, not that I understood what he meant quite by *"the Mystic Lover"*, but it is true, we must all try to do our share and play our part.'

So, together, they tried to sing what they could remember of the song. They sang it nine times eventually, after sorting out a few mistakes and harmonies:

I am the Mystic Lover
I call to your honey-filled heart

May you become intoxicated
May you play your part.

Amritah was in raptures, 'Oh, that was so lovely!' The others smiled. 'Let's begin our consultation.'

Ameya proceeded to draw out a route in the dusty ground then drew a rather wiggly version of the map of India.

He said, 'I had an old friend who onth showed me what our land looked like. I hope I got it right. We have to dethide how we will go thouth. May I jutht thay that it ith a very long way ath the crow flieth, as the thaying goeth.' That ith the direct way. Thtraight. Look!'

Adinah looked at the line that Ameya had just drawn right from the top of his map, straight down the middle making a dot at the other end somewhere in the South where he thought the Holy Hill might be.

'Umm, I am not sure that we can fly straight down just like that. It would be good if we could, but it is so very far. There will be lots of places that we will have to avoid, like cities and places where there is no water. We will have to make sure there is food available for everyone along the way too. We will have to feel our way as we go and we must listen to each member of our group. Are you sure that is what India looks like?' asked Amritah.

'Yeth, yeth. I am pretty thor it ith like that,' replied Amaya.

'Okay,' said Adinah, 'we need to look at the different places where we will have to go in order to reach our final destination. Let me think. Now, I have an idea. You know, not everyone of us is going to be able to fly for such long periods. We all know that it is a long way away and it will take us weeks, if not months to ever reach there. I suggest that we follow the railway line. The reason I say that is because when we get tired we can take a ride on the roof of the trains. Perhaps even stay on the tops all the time.'

'What a clever idea,' said Amritah. Adesah and Ameyah both nodded in agreement.

'Now how do we find out where to go first?'

'I know, I know,' said Adesah hopping up and down. 'From here, you will have to go directly to Delhi. I know the way and lots of trains go there, but you will have to go to *Dehra Dun* first as that is the nearest town from which the trains go.'

'Can't we find a train nearer here, Adinah?' ventured Amritah.

'Well, Rishikesh is on a branch line so we need to go to *Dehra Dun,*' Adinah said.

Up until now, Agnivalah hadn't said a word. He had been thinking seriously. He thought he had a distant relative, who lived in a place called *Katpadi* in the State of Tamil Nadu.

He said, 'No, I think the nearest station from here is in *Dehra Dun* so we must fly directly there. If we were to sit on a train to Delhi, then we will probably find one that's going south. There may be a relative of mine living down there somewhere, and when we get there, I could try and contact some of my own kind to see if he is still around. There aren't many of our kind left living down there, but if I can somehow make contact, he may be able to show us the way to the Holy Mountain which, I believe, is not very far away.'

'Great idea,' said Adesah. 'Shall we call the others and tell them our plan?'

'Yes do,' said Amritah.

Within five minutes, all had gathered together. Abhilasha having had a good sleep, was up and bouncing now.

'This is our plan,' said Amritah. She proceeded to explain what they had all discussed. Then she said, 'We rather liked that song that Ananta and Ajitah had dreamed about, so we decided to start our consultation by singing it together. We have almost learned it. It might be nice to end our consultation by singing it again. Would you all like to join us?' Of course, everybody agreed, so with a few mistakes here and there, they sang in unison.

What did it matter if there were? Their hearts were truly singing.

I am the Mystic Lover
I call to your honey-filled heart
May you become intoxicated
May you play your part.

Oh, what a heart-warming sight it was. The Nine had become truly united and now they were about to embark on the biggest journey of their lives.

Chapter Thirteen

'Let's go,' shouted Adesah, and at that moment they all rose into the air as if one single entity and flew into the distant sunset following Agnivalah and Adesah. All sang out

May you become intoxicated
May you play your part.

As they flew, Agnivalah slowly became aware of another bird flying close nearby. Yes, it was the spirit of his dearly loved wife. A wave of contentment and peace flowed inwardly through him. How happy he was.

'Oh, bless you, bless you for coming, my dearest,' he whispered. He knew without a doubt, that she had indeed passed over and her spirit had come to join him on this momentous journey. Now, he felt complete.

It was dark by the time they alighted on the top of a train that was slowly moving out of the station. Adesah said that he sensed it was moving in the right direction. It was crowded with people and baggage and a few were sitting on the rooftop but The Nine found an open-ended carriage where nobody was sitting. So, between the floor, an empty wicker basket and some railings, they each found a safe perch for the journey. No-one disturbed them. What good luck!

And so it was that the company of The Nine found themselves on the first stage of their incredible journey.

MAP OF THE JOURNEY AS DRAWN BY AMEYA

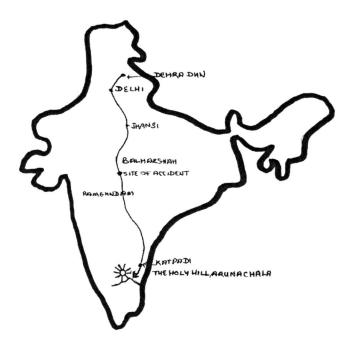

Chapter Fourteen

The next morning's sun found them all sleeping soundly. It wasn't until the train blew its whistle that any of them woke up.

'Good gracious,' said Adinah as he ruffled his bright green feathers and stretched out his wings.

'Wake up, wake up everybody. We have arrived!'

All jumped up, squawked, whistled and stretched in the smoke, commotion and babble of the busy station. Delhi at last.

Up they all flew into the city pollution. It was hard to breathe and little Alokah had a choking fit and nearly fell to the ground, but she kept going, thanks to the encouraging cluckings of Adinah who was flying just behind her. Eventually, they all rose above the clamour of the city to the clearer blue sky leaving behind the crowded station and noise.

'Adethah had been right,' thought Ameya as he flew higher and higher. 'He obviouthly hath an innate good thenthe of directhion which will therve uth all very well. God be praithed!'

It was Agnivalah who spoke next as he flew ahead of the others, 'We must take stock of our situation. I can just see a large water tank ahead. People are bathing there. Let us aim for that and find a spot to rest.' They all swooped down to a scrubbly little corner under a broken wall and kept out of sight.

'Oh, at last I can have a bath,' squealed Abhilasha and with a big splash, plunged straight into the corner of the tank. The others all followed suit.

'How divine!'

'This is heavenly!'

'Oh, that feels better!'

'How lovely to feel clean again.'

'Yippee!'

These and various other exclamations could be heard as all refreshed and gladdened their hearts in the water tank. Ten minutes later, all could be seen perching on various broken bricks in the scrubby little corner of the wall, stretching out their wings and generally pecking out any remaining dust particles in their feathers.

Amritah spoke aloud to everyone, 'So here we are in Delhi. We must make plans as soon as possible and find out where we have to go to reach the very far station called *Katpadi*. But first we must eat.'

Agnivalah then said, 'If you like, I am willing to explore the area. Adesah, will you come with me?'

'Of course. I would love to,' and off they both flew.

Much later on, when the sun was high in the sky, one by one, The Nine returned and gathered in the shady corner of the water tank.

Each had found pickings to eat and was ready for the next part of the journey.

Agnivalah and Adesah were the last to arrive, happy and thoroughly delighted with their news. They had flown back immediately to the station and discovered through a series of improbable events that a train was actually standing at the end of a line, waiting to leave for *Katpadi* the very next morning. This fact thrilled them both. What good fortune had dropped into their laps. A direct train! Using the rooftops of trains to reach their destination was proving to be a great idea. But it would still be a very long journey.

'Well,' said Agnivalah, 'it would be an impossible journey for us all if we were attempting to fly the distance. Why, who could possibly fly that far?'

'Yes, you are right,' said Adesah, 'but at least we will have done the major part of our journey by the time we arrive at *Katpadi*, won't we Agnivalah?'

Everybody was delighted to hear the news and for the rest of the day they prepared themselves, each in his or her unique way, for the forthcoming journey. It would be a long, hot and dusty journey and, if they had known it, they would have discovered it was the eleven-thirty, *Kerala Express* that they would be catching.

Chapter Fifteen

The next morning, after bathing and feeding, The Nine headed off in the direction of New Delhi station with Adesah and Agnivalah in front. Soon they found the train and flew near one of the rooftops.

'We shall never be able to sleep up here,' commented Ajitah. 'We shall be blown away. Let's go and find a better spot.' And so Ananta and Ajitah fluttered around to look for a better location.

This time, a place was found in a corner of an open carriage near the back of the train. How fortunate that trains often had an open carriage. Soon, everyone was sitting tight just as a warning bell went off making them all jump out of their skins. Then the engine started shunting out onto the correct bit of railway track.

'Phew, that was close,' said Ananta. 'But at least we are safely on our way again.'

'The journey seems so easy for us all,' said Ajitah.

'Yes,' said Agnivalah. 'The fun will begin when I try to find my relative once we've arrived in *Katpadi*. But at least we can all settle down now for a good long trip. It's going to take us more than a couple of days to get there.'

Amritah started to hum to herself and before long, all the others were singing along with her.

I am the Mystic Lover
I call to your honey-filled heart
May you become intoxicated
May you play your part.

Long after everyone had stopped singing and each was lost in his or her own thoughts, Amritah contemplated events from the very beginning of her journey. She had been a shy young bird when she had first left Virbhadra. She thought about her family and friends and how they had encouraged her to take the trip. She missed them a lot and they were often on her mind.

'I love them all so much. I hope they aren't missing me, but I bet they are. I will have so much to tell them if I get to see them. Shall I ever see them again?' Right there and then she had a little weep, 'Oh, I do hope I shall see them all again one day. I wonder ...'

Amritah's uncle, her mother's elder brother, had been the famous Raji-B whom she loved very much. He had shared some good stories with her when she was small. To her, he was the very embodiment of a divine soul: kind-hearted and generous almost to a fault, but not long before she had left on this journey, he had passed away. She had felt so alone and sad to lose such a loving relative and friend. Several times he had mentioned that a message would come from afar especially for her which would be life-changing.

'Well,' she thought to herself, 'I really do feel that this *is* a special call for me and it certainly is changing my life! I have never been so far away from my home before and yet I don't feel afraid. How is it possible? This is a very lovely group I have found myself part of and they make me feel so ... so ... content.' She suddenly felt a wave of emotion catch her throat and she started to weep. 'Yes ...' she thought to herself, ... 'yes, I do feel more courageous

thanks to all the encouragement from the others!' Amritah thought about Amarah, the Deathless One. 'He was a strange bird, that one,' she mused. 'How was it that he could disappear into thin air, just like that? This indeed, is a strange journey.'

Meanwhile, the train had accelerated out of the station and found its own smooth rhythm. *Chug-a-dug-a, chug-a-dug-a, chug-a-dug-a, chug-a-dug-a.*

Then Amritah started to think about Amarah's message. He had sung a beautiful song. It was a famous poem.

'Now, how did it go?'

Chug-a-dug-a, chug-a-dug-a, chug-a-dug-a, chug-a-dug-a. The train rattled on.

'Ah, ummm...yes, something like ...'
then it all came back to her.

Listen to the Exhortation of the Dawn!
Look to this Day!
For it is Life, the very Life of Life.
In its brief course lie all the
Verities and Realities of your Existence.
The Bliss of Growth,
The Glory of Action,
The Splendor of Beauty;
For Yesterday is but a Dream,
And Tomorrow is only a Vision;
But Today well lived makes
Every Yesterday a Dream of Happiness,
And every Tomorrow a Vision of Hope.
Look well therefore to this Day!
Such is the Salutation of the Dawn!

For a long time she pondered on the
words. She continued to think long and hard.
These words were dancing before her eyes. They
illuminated her mind. They wove a magic spell
into her loving and tender heart. Eventually, a
question began to form in her mind.

Look to this Day!
For it is Life, the very Life of Life.

She thought: 'What does this *very Life of Life* mean?'
For Yesterday is but a Dream,
And Tomorrow is only a Vision;
But Today well lived...

'How can I make my life *Today well lived'*...she mused...

For a long time, these fragments of the song went round and round inside her mind just like the train was saying *chug-a-dug-a, chug-a-dug-a, chug-a-dug-a, chug-a-dug-a.*

Then with a sudden jolt, her question arose. She really wanted to know. To know *why* this life is as it is.

'We are all so different. We all experience life in so many different ways, but... For me to live my life well, I have to ask myself *Who am I and why am I here?'*

She sat quietly contemplating this profound question as if an answer might just happen to come at any moment...

Adinah sat for a long time on a corner railing of the coach, mesmerised by the *chug-a-dug-a, chug-a-dug-a, chug-a-dug-a, chug-a-dug-a* sound of the train. He watched the world as it flashed past him.

'A rather grey and bewildering world,' he thought. *Is it the world that is passing me by or am I passing the world by?* Why, that is a funny thought, he pondered and chuckled to himself. He had made many journeys on his own, but this was quite unique.

'Fancy travelling on a train. I certainly have often followed train lines in my travels, but never thought of actually sitting on one. Well I never!' And again he started to chuckle to himself. Then he became a little more serious, as he wondered whether he would be able to complete the journey. He was elderly now and he didn't want to be a burden to anyone. He had never been further south than the outskirts of

Rishikesh. His excursions mostly took him up north when he went in search of rare herbs. Yes, he was used to travelling but he wondered how he would cope with the heat as he had heard it was very hot in the South.

'All I want is a bit of peace and quiet,' he thought to himself. 'What is an old chap like me doing on this trip, anyway? I would just like to find a nice, quiet spot where I can spend the rest of my days in contemplation and meditation.'

He thought back to his family and the Virbhadra days which were sunny and relatively peaceful. But he had never quite got over leaving Mussoorie. He had been the happiest bird alive, living up there. 'Oh well,' he thought, 'at least they are all happy.' Then he settled back into the *chug-a-dug-a, chug-a-dug-a, chug-a-dug-a, chug-a-dug-a* of the train.

Adinah fell asleep for a while, then woke up as a big thought entered his mind. It was the thought of Amarah, the singing nightingale. A fragment of his message entered Adinah's mind:

... each one of you is being called upon to fulfill your destiny ... 'Is this my destiny? I suppose it must be, otherwise I wouldn't be here, would I?' *... you may become a source of strength to others who are very much in need of your skills in these difficult times.* 'Oh yes,' he thought, 'I will do my best to be of help to whoever needs it. I hope I live long enough to be of some use.' *... another journey...to a sacred mountain in the South of India ...* 'Why in the South? I wonder what is there. There is some hill. A Holy Hill? He did mention the name of somebody there, too. Now what was it? ... Ah yes, Anadi, that's what it was. Amarah had said that this Anadi would *lead us to our heart's desire ... to understand the truth of our existence* ... or something like that. Well, that would be good. I would then have something to meditate on, wouldn't I? Umm, okay. I am looking forward to meeting Anadi and perhaps he will guide me?'

He then thought of the question he might ask if he ever got to meet Anadi.

'Is it the world that is passing me by, or

am I passing the world by? I don't seem to be able to come up with an answer myself.'

And so Adinah continued to muse on these thoughts and the singing train went on *chug-a-dug-a, chug-a-dug-a, chug-a-dug-a, chug-a-dug-a.*

Ajitah and Ananta had found a cosy corner on the floor of the train carriage. They had been billing and cooing and trying to wrap their wings around each other. They truly were in love. These two birds were very pretty to look at and their bodies had exquisite dark grey beauty spots painted all over their wings in a very artistic manner. After some time, the *chug-a-dug-a, chug-a-dug-a, chug-a-dug-a, chug-a-dug-a* had lulled them into a semi-comatose state, sending them off to sleep. Eventually, the sun moved and their little shady corner was shady no more. They both woke up in a sweat.

'Good gracious, it is getting jolly hot,' panted Ajitah. 'I shall bake to death down here.' Ananta hopped across the floor to the other side of the carriage where there was a little shade and Ajitah quickly joined him. 'Phew, that's better. It is going to get hotter and hotter the further south we go, isn't it?' she added. Ananta agreed by nodding his head. He felt too hot even to speak.

Chug-a-dug-a, chug-a-dug-a, chug-a-dug-a, chug-a-dug-a went the train and the two love birds listened to the sound of the wheels on the tracks as they went along. Both of them in their own way began thinking about their shared dream of a huge mountain that rose out of the plain with a cave on its side and a tree beside it. Then they remembered the beautiful voice that had spoken to them of love and told them that they were very special and must become *True Lovers.*

'He sang so sweetly,' sighed Ajitah. 'Oh my.'

Ananta hummed to himself. 'Yes, my darling. You and I are the reflection of Love. We must discover what he meant by *True Lovers.*'

Chapter Sixteen

Ananta loved to think.

This was his favourite occupation, apart from wooing Ajitah. He thought back to his nesting days with his two younger brothers.

'I wonder what they are doing now? Making families? I wonder how my parents are? I am glad they liked Ajitah. Yes, I am very fortunate to have such a loving wife too, and here we are sitting on a train with a bunch of different kinds of birds all heading south. Life is strange!' he thought. 'I like these folk, they certainly are an interesting bunch. All of us seem to be following the same ideal. Is this all a dream? Is this real? What is real?' he carried on thinking. He thought about Alokah and her dream of a sacred Hill in the South.

'Is that where we are going?' he wondered. He thought it was. Then he thought about Anadi, the friend of Amarah 'I wonder what he will be like and will he be found easily?' Then he looked across at Amritah sitting with Abhilasha who was dozing in another corner. 'Amritah is a good leader. She really cares about us all and is very fair. I do like her. I wonder if we need to take turns. She hadn't wanted to be the leader at all and she may like a change.' Again, he thought about his questions: 'Is this all a dream? Is this real? What is real?'

Meanwhile, Ajitah stared up into the sky. She was watching a small cloud of smoke float by. Then some migrating birds flew in formation high up in the sky. She had never been far from her own home although her parents had been great wanderers. This was a big journey for her but she took it in her stride. She liked the idea of seeing different places and was thankful that Ananta was with her. She looked at him and smiled to herself. How she loved him. He was so ... gorgeous! Her heart skipped a beat.

'How lovely that we are both here on this trip together.' She looked around at each of the others in turn. 'These are the most delightful friends,' she thought. 'I never dreamed that I would be travelling and living in the company of such a colourful group. I wonder where we will all end up. Will I see my family again? I do hope so. I shall want to tell them about everything that has happened. They won't believe me probably.' Then her thoughts wandered to thinking about Amarah and his amazing disappearance. 'No-one would ever believe that!' she reflected. 'I wonder where he is now ...' She thought about the story he had told them, about the spider's web. 'That was such an amazing story. All those dew drops on his web, each reflecting the same thing in every one. I liked it best when he said ... now ... what was it ..? Oh yes ... he said, whatever he did, said, or thought, and whatever everyone else did, said or thought, would all be reflected in all other dew drops and he said something about being eternal. What was it? Ummm ... oh yes, I've got it. He said if we are all reflected in the myriad dew drops then we must affect each other and that proved we are eternal, or something like that. What was it? Something about being just *one* happening and being eternally one. Oh, what was it? I can't remember exactly. I shall have to ask Ananta later when he is awake.' A question kept going round her head, 'Am I eternal? Am I eternal?' After a while, she resumed her occupation of staring up at the sky as if it might provide her with an answer.

Ameya was sitting bolt upright on a railing, hugging the wall closely so as to not be blown off whilst watching the passing landscape. His eyes could scarcely believe what they saw all around him: such a big world out there. It was breathtaking. His mind wandered back and forth and he thought of the company he was in.

'A thtrange bunch, but very noble and kindly. If it wathn't for Abhilasha, I would never be here.' Then he cast a glance in her direction. She was asleep. 'Thith trip will be the making of her,' he reflected fondly. 'I do hope thow.' Then he started thinking about something Amarah had said in his talk. He had mentioned that the *heart and the mind must work together in order to have balance and justice in society... When we see harmony and peace all around us, what is happening?* 'It ith true. The heart and mind mutht work together. I agree with that. All thowth beingth out there, millionth of them. Now, if everyone uthed their head *and* heart together there would be no more fighting. We would have a peathful and loving world. What kind of world would that be like? What can *I* do about that? How can *I* change?' then he started thinking about his 'I'. 'What ith thith *I* that I call mythelf? I am me, but where ith my *I?* I don't theem to be able to find it. Umm. Then *I* mutht be my body. No, it can't be. Then it mutht be my mind. Umm. Could be. Maybe my mind ith a tool for my *I?* But what *ith* thith *I?* Maybe it ith my perthonality? Thith bit which ith called Ameya. Yeth, that mutht be it. But who created it? Oh dear, I am getting confewthd.'

Chapter Seventeen

As Ameya sat brooding, an enormous bird dropped out of the sky and sat beside him on the railing, casting a huge shadow. Poor Ameya nearly jumped out of his skin.

'Oh my, oh, ah, er, oh dear, er, I nearly fell off my perch. Who ... who ... are you?' he stuttered.

Do not be afraid, the big bird said. *I have been around for a very long time. I heard your thoughts. I could not help hearing them. You want to know some answers, is that correct?*

Ameya looked intently at this newcomer. He seemed a very ancient eagle. In fact, he looked rather like that eagle who had a family nest in the tree where he lived, in Virbhadra.

'Are you, are you ... no, you can't be,'

said the crow. 'I heard a tale onthe about an old eagle who had lived a very long time before in my home tree in Virbhadra. He had become enlightened ... whatever that meanth.'

Indeed, I am the spirit of that eagle. I live in all the worlds and I can fly anywhere and everywhere I please in order to give assistance wherever it is needed. I was very happy living in Virbhadra. It is a very special place. You are fortunate to have lived there. You are very blessed. My descendants live there now. I was attracted by your warm heart and the company you are travelling with. Very interesting ...very interesting! Are you the one called Ameya?

'Yeth I am. How ... how ... did you know?'

The visitor became remote and silent.

'Can the otherth thee you?' asked Ameya.

Not neccessarily. Only if they want to. Let me tell you something. It might help to answer some of your questions.

Ameya was all ears. He was enthralled by the presence of this unusual visitor. He emanated a brilliant radiance that almost seemed to burn his feathers.

He asked, 'Do you have a name?'

The eagle carried on speaking, ignoring Ameya's question.

Everyone is aware of the Self, but not very clearly. It is not distinct. Sometimes you will have a 'sense' of it when you are quiet or not thinking much about anything, but at other times, the worldly business will cloud your mind and senses, and the Self will cease to be clear. The Self is that bit of you which is the 'real' you. The 'eternal' bit of you. The bit that never dies. You always exist. You were asking yourself about your 'I'. This 'I' cannot be pointed at. It cannot be fathomed by your mind. This 'I' just 'is'. 'I Am' is the name of the Divine in you which is now manifesting as a crow. This 'I' is Absolute Being. It is not that little personality called Ameya. 'I' is the Self. It is God, it is also Buddha nature, it is ONLY the Divine. By knowing the Self, God will become known. God is none other than the Self. Eternal in the past and eternal in the future.

The eagle became quiet. He sat very still. Ameya noticed that he did not move at all on the railing. He did not even wobble about like he himself did, to keep his balance. He was absolutely immovable.

The train's continual *chug-a-dug-a, chug-a-dug-a, chug-a-dug-a, chug-a-dug-a* interrupted *Ameya's* thoughts.

'Goth, I feel very privileged,' he thought to himself and just as he was thinking, the eagle spoke.

'If you ever need me, just call me, and I will come. Goodbye.' And he was gone as quickly as he had come.

'But, what ...what ...' Ameyah didn't manage to finish his question, '...what name will

I call you by? Oh, dear,' he thought, 'Maybe I will justht know what to call him if I should need him.' Just at that moment, he *knew* that he would.

Chapter Eighteen

Alokah had not said anything for a long time. In fact, she had remained at the back of the group. Nobody had noticed her much. She felt a little forlorn but she was used to it. She had never really known her parents, as they had died when she was young and had no other family that she knew of. The Nine had become her new, adoptive family. This was such a daunting journey, but her heart was full of peace. Dear Agnivalah always kept an eye on her. She did not know it then, but Amritah was also watching over her closely as she knew that Alokah had very special qualities which would one day show themselves.

'Perhaps she could be the next leader?' Amritah pondered.

Alokah had found a little shady corner just below the railing where Ameya was sitting. She had seen the big shadow of the visiting eagle and she had heard every word that he had spoken.

'Those words are very similar to the ones I heard in my dream,' she thought. 'I am returning home. I can just feel it. Yes, I am returning Home. The Home of my heart. This visitor is calling me home. Home! Oh, I am so excited.' At that thought, she immediately called across to Ameya.

'Ameya, Ameya, I heard everything that the great bird said to you. You know, it is the same voice that was in my dream. It is the voice of Truth, I tell you. I am so excited. I can't believe it. Oh, I am so happy. I am going Home Ameya. Do you believe it? Can you feel it? I think that we are *all* going Home. How lucky we all are. We are the chosen ones. I do feel that. Do you remember when I talked about my vision and I had seen a beautiful rainbow being? I had such a strong feeling that we would all be looked after by a great loving force. I reckon it is that big eagle. He must be the One who is looking over us as we make this journey, don't you think so, Ameya? I really am very happy.'

Ameya looked over to Alokah in total surprise. He had never seen her so animated. She

was looking positively ... dare he think it ...
Divine.

'Yeth, yeth, my dear Alokah. You are
very blethed. Indeed, I am feeling very happy
too.'

Alokah, changing the subject, said
'Now how long will it be before we reach our
destination Ameya?'

At that point, Adesah, who had heard
Alokah mention the word *journey,* quickly
hopped with a merry skip across the carriage
floor to join them in their conversation. He also
wanted to know how long the journey would
take.

'Yeth, I think it will take a good two
dayth from thtart to finish.' Said Ameya. 'Let'th
think. Ummm ... anyone good at math around
here?

'Yes, I am quite,' said Adesah.

'Umm,' said Ameya. 'Hum ... hum ...
hum, we left, *New Delhi* at eleven-thirty thith

morning and we have to path by a few plathes. *Mathura, Agra, Gwalior, Jhanthi, ... ummm ... Bhopal, Nagpur, Ramgundam, Nellore, Tirupati, Chittor ... ah ... umm, yeth and finally to Katpadi.* There are otherth but thowth are the oneth I found out about.'

'Let me think,' said Adesah. 'If *Katpadi* is our destination, then we should allow a hundred and something miles between each place that the train goes through. It might be about fourteen or fifteen hundred miles or so, and I reckon that we should reach *Katpadi* in ... um, let's see ... um, yes, about thirty-six hours, or a few more. That means we could reach our destination in two or three days ... I think that is right. Then we shall arrive in the middle of the night.' He let out a long whistle.

Alokah was delighted to hear that news.

'Oh,' she said, 'I will soon be Home.' And she smiled to herself, a very big smile of inner knowing. She was at peace with herself. Her only thought was, How soon, how soon?

Adesah hopped back to his resting place and thought about how his life had been transformed over these last few days. He had been so keen to go on this trip. Yes, he was loving every bit of this amazing journey and he liked the company of the other birds.

'Quite a bright lot, really.' he thought. He had been so happy when his friends had also wanted to go with him. Then he thought about the fact that he hadn't told many stories lately. But at times, he hoped that he had cheered up the company of friends with his bright comments and chirpy songs.

Chapter Nineteen

Adesah now turned his thoughts to more serious matters. He had been impressed with Amarah's talk. He loved his songs, his manner and in fact, everything about him. He was dignified too. Adesah thought about how Amarah had just disappeared in a ball of light.

'Wow, that was so amazing!' he thought to himself. 'What a show!' Then, as he sat reflecting, a little song floated into his mind. It was the song that Amarah had sung just before he had disappeared. He was impressed that he could recall it, because the tune was rather quite catchy. 'Such a kind and loving look he gave me too. I shall never forget that,' and he thought about what Amarah had said: *Love is the key. Love, love and more love. Think it, express it, show it and give it your attention at all times and in all places. Give it willingly to all whom you may meet along the way especially to those who will surely test you and cause you pain.*

Agnivalah was enjoying the ride. He had found a soft bit of old cloth that had been left on the ground and was sitting right in the middle of it. It slithered around a bit as the train moved, but after arranging it near a corner, he was able to wedge himself in and make a comfortable seat for himself. His wife's spirit spent more and more time with him and he found having her around a great source of comfort. When he talked with her, sometimes she responded but at other times she did not. He always felt a great love emanating from her presence. He thought about the sort of life-style they had shared together in their home in Virbhadra. It had been a rather meaningless social round. Now, he felt he was really listening to his heart.

'Because I am listening to my heart, perhaps that is why she is with me now,' he thought. 'It's a hard lesson to learn. I should have listened to that inner voice more when she was alive. But I suppose everything has its own time and that is now. Goodness, yes, the time is *now*. No good thinking about the past. That has all gone. And Amarah had sung that beautiful and inspiring song for us all to realise just that!

For Yesterday is but a Dream,
And To-morrow is only a Vision;
But To-day well lived makes
Every Yesterday a Dream of Happiness,
And every Tomorrow a Vision of Hope.

'Oh yes, I must live in the *now* and that is what my heart says. How does one go about that?' he thought. 'Well, I am sitting here on this funny clackety-clack train. I have nothing to do except wait for the next stop and go and find something to eat. I wonder if I will find my relative? I hope he is still alive. Well, if I am to live in the *now,* that means I must live in this present moment. Okay, so no more worrying about this or that or the other. It will all turn out for the best, I am sure. This group seem so blessed. I feel blessed. Fancy having my wife here too.' Agnivalah felt contented and at peace. 'Maybe I will find out more about living in the *Now* when we arrive at our destination?' With this thought in his mind, off he went to sleep.

Abhilasha was still sitting beside

Amritah. She had woken up and now felt completely rested.

'Amritah is a delight,' she thought to herself. 'I love her!'

Chug-a-dug-a, chug-a-dug-a, chug-a-dug-a, chug-a-dug-a went the train.

She stretched out her wings and shook her face. She felt *so* much better.

'Thank goodness,' she thought as she listened to the sound of the train and felt the gentle swaying motion. She settled down again to review the past few days. Abhilasha thought about the meaningless activities she had engaged in during her life. Momentary glimpses of what she *thought* was happiness. They seemed shabby in contrast to what was happening now. Her life was beginning to have some meaning and seemed to be getting into some sort of order. It felt fulfilling. She now felt part of the great universal impulse. 'And it is all thanks to Amritah who has helped me get through it with her unconditional love. I would never have managed without her. Bless her!'

She thought to herself, 'I haven't been a very nice person so far in my life. I have been selfish and greedy. I have only really cared about myself. I even used to steal food from others. I was deceitful. This is terrible!' Then she started to cry. Amritah, who was sitting nearby, moved closer to her. She understood exactly what Abhilasha must be going through and could feel her pain.

'Oh, I have been such a selfish person. Can I ever be forgiven? I do so want to change my ways. I want to become *divine,* whatever that may mean. I know it must be something good, and that is all I want to be. I want to be kind and good. Ameya has always believed in me. He has been so good to me too, over the years, and I haven't always been very nice to him ... Oh ... oh ... oh.'

Amritah stretched out her wing and placed it softly across Abhilasha's back. Then she began to sing softly, a gently lullaby. The tears stopped and Abhilasha became quiet. Then Amritah sang the song that Amarah, the

nightingale had sung just before he made his
spectacular disappearance.

This is love:
To fly to heaven,
Every moment to rend a hundred veils;
At first instance,
To break away from breath –
First step, to renounce feet;
To disregard this world,
To see only that
Which you yourself have seen.

Abhilasha sat entranced with Amritah's
beautiful rendition of this famous song. Now she
felt better.

'Thank you, thank you, dear Amritah.
How can I ever thank you for your kindness? Is
it possible to change ourselves? I mean, can I
ever become *divine?* Can I be forgiven? Can I
change myself? Can I become more loving
towards others? Oh, I do hope so.

Amritah spoke softly, 'All things are

possible, my dear. Sometimes during our lives, we get a feeling or a nudge that is meaningful and important for each one of us. That is why we are all on this journey. We are being given a little nudge, don't you think? Why have we been given this opportunity? I think it is because we all *do* truly want to change ourselves. I also believe that we will be totally transformed when we reach our destination and then it won't matter any more how our lives have been because all will be forgiven in that moment. I believe that we are being given this gift, this journey of a lifetime because we may have done something good in the past.'

'I hope you are right my friend, and thank you again,' sighed Abhilasha. Both sat quietly side by side.

Chug-a-dug-a, chug-a-dug-a, chug-a-dug-a, chug-a-dug-a, the train rattled on.

Chapter Twenty

The countryside flew by, towns and cities flew by. The trees, the hills, the valleys, vast expanses of scrubland waste, water tanks, the highways and byways, all flew past the companions. The distance was huge. The sky, fathomless in its blueness: an eternity. The comings and goings of humanity. The doings of all creatures great and small. All flew by. The train rumbled on and on and on in its determination to reach the goal. *Chug-a-dug-a, chug-a-dug-a, chug-a-dug-a, chug-a-dug-a* a timeless moment.

Eventually, a loud whistle blew and the train ground to a halt. They had reached some place. Loud voices rang out. There was an urgency of coming and going. It was hot. The sun was high in the sky, and the companions had not eaten for a long time. They also needed water.

The Nine flew onto the railings and looked about them. They had stopped in a good place.

'Hey, look! There's a large temple over there,' shouted Adesah, 'let's go and explore. There should be a nice water tank nearby and perhaps we shall have time to find some food.'

This had not been the first stop the train had made on the long journey south, but it was the first time that all felt they needed some refreshment. It had taken short stops in different places all the way down the line thus far.

'Do you think we have time, and where are we?' asked Amritah.

Adinah ruffled his green feathers and offered to go and explore the area. 'I'll go along with Adesah and find out.'

Amritah then asked everybody what they thought of that plan.

'Yes, yes. Good idea.'

'Good, then come back quickly and safely,' said Amritah. And off the two friends flew.

The station was crowded. It was all very confusing and noisy and the two friends were glad to be clear of the chaos. They were back in less than five minutes with plenty to report.

'Yes, there is water and food near the temple complex. And the train isn't leaving for another two hours! There's some story going around, that just a mile down the line, part of the track is damaged and now it is being repaired. They are refuelling and are adding some more carriages for some reason. We have lots of time. This is *Jhansi Junction*,' reported Adinah.

This was good news for everyone, so off they all flew in a colourful flurry of feathers and headed towards the temple water tank, plunging in up to their necks as quickly as they could. Ahhh, the cool, clear water was like nectar to this little band of pilgrims. They soaked themselves in the waters for what seemed like hours, then off they went to look for food. It was agreed that they would all return to the side of the water tank once they had finished eating. Consultation: this was the way to work as a team. Yes, consultation was how they all agreed to meet and part and meet up again.

Agnivalah was impressed with the way this little group worked things out. First, each had his or her say and every word was listened to and honoured however insignificant it might have been considered by any member of the group. Then they acted on the majority view, which seemed to be what everyone wanted anyway. It was the responsibility of all to look after each other and it worked.

Amritah, who was still the leader saw to it that whenever anyone left the group, for whatever reason, they should go in pairs or threes and let the rest know where they could be found in case of need.

A while later, chanting could be heard coming from inside the temple. It was beautiful, thought Amritah as she sat watching the surface of the water moving gently in the breeze. She felt clean and full: a good feeling! She wondered if someone else would now like to take the responsibility of being the leader. One by one, the company of friends reassembled on the side of the tank. Not far away, a *sadhu* in an orange loin cloth was taking a bath, saying his prayers and he sang softly to himself: a peaceful scene.

'That feels so much better!' said the two love birds together as they flapped their wings and laughed. Ajitah and Ananta were as happy as ever.

'They seem to be the very embodiment of love,' thought Amritah. 'A joy to behold!'

Amritah called the group together and asked if anyone else would like to take the responsibility now of being leader for the next part of the journey. Nobody spoke. Nobody volunteered.

'Well,' she said, 'I think it is only fair that we take it in turns. Why, it was Ananta who had suggested that in the first place.'

'Then perhaps Ananta should be the next leader,' commented Adesah.

The discussions went back and forth as all good consultations do and eventually it was agreed that Ajitah and Ananta would be joint leaders. Everyone was happy with that decision and the consultation ended with lots of hurrays, thank yous and big hugs for Amritah for all she had done, followed by a loud flapping of their wings and stampings of their feet, all in good-hearted agreement. She had proved to be a most caring leader.

And so it was that The Nine grew closer together. They were truly beginning to respect each other and looking at the good qualities that each had to offer rather than dwelling on their weaknesses. The loving co-leadership of Ajitah and Ananta would help to cement further the unity of the group.

Ananta then spoke in his best possible voice, 'Thank you for believing in us. We shall do our very best to serve the group, won't we, Ajitah?' His young voice giving away his age.

'Yes we will, my dearest. And now we must head back to the train as we have been away quite a long time. We don't want to miss it now, do we?'

Once they had arrived back at the train,

their carriage had gone. 'Oh no,' said Ajitah, 'we had better search for another one.'

Adesah quickly responded and flew up to a beam in the ceiling of the station. He could see three new carriages that had been added to the train. The end one was empty.

'Yippee, yes, follow me.' He whistled to the others as he flew down. 'Follow me.'

The carriage was a little rusty in places but it would suit The Nine. It was partly covered and full of large hessian sacks of grain. It was open at the far end.

'This is a perfect place for us,' said Ananta. 'Thank you, dear Adesah.'

Chapter Twenty-one

By late evening, The Nine had found comfortable places to rest and ended up having a jolly good night's sleep. Nothing disturbed them. Just the sound of the train rolling along the tracks lulled their senses and brought a calm peace to each of their hearts. *Chug-a-dug-a, chug-a-dug-a, chug-a-dug-a, chug-a-dug-a.*

This train, unbeknown to The Nine, was what was called, a *through* train. That meant that the train would only stay for a few minutes at each station along the way, and nobody would have to change to catch another train. This was a fortunate thing because these friends had no notion of the concept of having to change trains. It was just fortuitous that they had had such a long stop in *Jhansi Junction.*

Early the next morning, just as the stars were fading and the sun began to climb above the horizon, The Nine were woken up by a jolting and crashing ahead of them.

They were all knocked off their perches and they made a terrible racket of shrieks of surprise between them all. Quickly and calmly, Ananta and Ajitah together called the rest of the friends to keep close to each other at any price, then the two of them flew up onto the roof of the carriage to see what was happening. Ahead, the front of the train had veered off part of the track and was lying on its side. The engine driver was on the ground beside it. People were running around screaming and causing a terrible hullabaloo and there was a lot of black smoke coming out of the engine room.

'Oh, my goodness,' said Ajitah. 'What has happened?' Then they saw that an elephant had crossed the line. The engine driver had slammed on his brakes, but he had not been fast enough, so the train engine had glanced off the elephant's back leg and landed on its side. At that very moment, the elephant, who had been pushed over by the impact, was in the process of trying to stand up.

'Oh, I am so glad he seems to be all right. It looks like he's up, but he's limping. Oh dear, do you think he will be okay, Ananta?'

186

Ananta was trying to support Ajitah with his wing rather unsuccessfully. Several people ran to help the driver. He seemed stunned but not injured. In fact, people had a number of minor injuries, but no-one had died thank goodness. A lot were in shock, including The Nine. Ananta and Ajitah made their way back down to the rest and informed them of what had happened.

'Well, it looks like we could be in for a long stop here,' said Ananta as he looked around at the others who were a little knocked about but had incurred no serious injuries. 'Are you are all okay?' he asked.

'Yeth, yeth, we are a bit bruithed, but otherwithe, we theem to be fine,' ventured Ameya.

Little Alokah called out and said, 'Let's go and see if we can do something.'

'Don't be silly,' muttered Adesah in a rather exasperated tone of voice, then quite forgetting himself added, 'How can we possibly help? We are only birds!'

'We could sing and make the people feel happy,' suggested Alokah.

Ameya suddenly remembered the eagle that had visited him.

He said, 'Shh, just for a moment plethe. I shall try and communicate with thomeone who might be able to help us.' Alokah instantly knew whom he was trying to call. All fell silent. Within a few moments, a whirring of mighty wings descended causing a big shadow to cover them all for a second. The spirit eagle had come.

'Bleth you for coming, my friend,' said Ameya, 'thank you for hearing me.'

Now, all the friends could see him clearly. The others were a little afraid because he was so huge, but soon realised that this was a friend who had come to help them and was emanating pure Love. He looked around at the company of birds and sensed their awe of him:

I come because your friend called me. I see that there has been a big accident. Do not be afraid,' the eagle said. 'You will all be fine. All the other passengers will be all right too, though it will take some time to clear up the mess. The driver will be taken away shortly as he is in shock, and a new engine and driver will arrive later. The elephant is fine and has gone. He is hardly injured and will recover from the shock. Stay near the carriage. Some grain has fallen out of a couple of bags. Perhaps you may eat some of that if you are hungry. Water is just over there. And he pointed to a spot off on the right and down a small slope.

'Please, kind sir, where are we?' asked Ajitah.

You are between Balharshah and Ramgundam in the State of Maharashtra,' he said. *'You are all well on your way. Be happy. Love and support each other and you will arrive safely.* And off he flew.

'Well,' said Alokah to Ameya. 'How did you call him?'

'I jutht thought of him, called to him in my mind and I vithualithed hith form. That ith all,' said Ameya.

'Very good. You did well,' she added.

It was to be a very long wait as it turned out. The new engine driver didn't arrive until later that evening. The Nine found water to drink and most of them enjoyed the grain that had fallen on the floor of the carriage. The eagle was right and there had also been plenty of time for seeking out food elsewhere.

Eventually, everybody was back on board and ready to go. By the time the train was moving again, it was well past sunset and The Nine settled down for the night.

'All's well that ends well,' sighed Abhilasha who was now sitting beside Ameya and fanning her face with a wing. 'Gosh it is so hot here. I hope we will survive!'

'Ameya, you did well calling that big eagle. He seems so wise. When did you meet him?' And so it was that Ameya kindly told her the whole story of how he had appeared to him. He told her of the message the spirit eagle had brought to him through his own self-enquiry.

He said, 'the thpirit eagle thaid to me, *The Self is that bit of you which is the 'real' you. The 'eternal' bit of you. The bit that never dies. You always exist.'* Imagine that!' He continued, *This 'I' cannot be pointed at. It cannot be fathomed by your mind. This 'I' just 'is',* and he altho thaid that, *'I Am' is the name of the Divine in you which is now manifesting as a crow. This 'I' is Absolute Being. It is not that little personality called Ameya. 'I' is the Self. It is God, the Divine. By knowing the Self, God will become known.* 'We are eternal beingth Abhilasha! Ithn't that incredible?'

Abhilasha was greatly moved by what Ameya was telling her. She wanted to believe him and almost could, but ... well, she would think about it all ... then off she went to sleep.

Chapter Twenty-two

The two love birds were wrapped up in each other's feathers happily billing and cooing softly to each other.

'You know, Ananta, we shall leave the train tomorrow morning if my calculations are right. I heard someone say that it would take about fifteen hours or so to get to *Katpadi,* and that is where we are going, isn't it?'

'Yes, my love. It is.'

'Then we will see our joint dream realised, won't we? I am excited about that.'

'Yes,' said Ananta, 'that will be very interesting, I think.'

'Agnivalah has a relative living near there doesn't he?'said Ajitah. 'I hope he finds him. That will be exciting too, won't it? We will have to fly the last bit, won't we? Will he show us the way?'

'Darling, I don't know. You have too many questions. Let's go to sleep. We shall need all our strength for tomorrow.'

'Of course, I love you my dearest.'

'I love you too, night night.'

Agnivalah was sitting near to Adinah who asked, 'Well, my dear friend, did you say you have a relative living near ... where was it?'

'*Katpadi,*' answered Agnivalah, 'I have a distant relative who lives over that side. A second cousin or something. I met him only once before, but he has kept in touch from time to time with some members of my family. I hope to locate him once we arrive there. It would be truly wonderful if I can find him. He might know the way to the Holy Mountain.'

'That would be very helpful to our group if you are able to find him,' Adinah said. 'So far, we have travelled in relative comfort. Nobody has got sick or injured. That in itself is a miracle.'

194

'It is indeed,' answered Agnivalah.

'Will you go alone in search of your relative?'

'Yes, I think I might have to.' But then Agnivalah looked slightly to one side and saw his beloved spirit wife there with him.

'I shall be fine,' he said, knowing that he would not be quite so alone.

Amritah, Adesah and Alokah were resting together. Adesah was singing softly and rocking himself at the same time.

He said, 'Alokah, I am sorry, I was very rude to you earlier today. Please forgive me. I was feeling a little bit stressed by everything and it ... well ... it just came out before I realised what I was saying.'

'Don't worry, Adesah. I haven't given it a second's thought. But let me say something. I believe that we birds *can* do a lot to help others. We can sing from our hearts, and that cheers people up for a start.'

195

'Yes, it is true. And you have a very sweet voice Alokah. You are very pretty to look at, too.' And then he winked at her.

'Oh you are a cheeky one,' blushed Alokah, and they all laughed.

Then Amritah said, 'Tomorrow is a big day for us all. We shall be arriving in *Katpadi* in the morning and Agnivalah has a relative living near there. Let us hope he finds him. It is the end of our free ride and we will all have to have strength to fly the last bit of the journey. I have to say that I am feeling very excited about it.'

Alokah nodded and said, 'I can't believe that I might see the mountain of my dream at last. I wonder if it is?'

Soon, all three were fast asleep and not a sound came from any corner of the carriage save the *chug-a-dug-a, chug-a-dug-a, chug-a-dug-a, chug-a-dug-a* of the train as it rattled on relentlessly.

Chapter Twenty-three

A blanket of deepest indigo embraced The Nine. The star-spangled sky with a thin crescent moon on the ascendant made a befitting blanket. A warm breeze whispered of fragrant holiness and greatness into their minds. All slept soundly and restfully. The train ran smoothly on. *Chug-a-dug-a, chug-a-dug-a, chug-a-dug-a, chug-a-dug-a.* As they slept, a luminous presence enveloped them, uniting them, weaving strength and fortitude into each one's heart. Yes, this precious company were indeed being watched over. The great spirit eagle had flown into all their dreams. He had sent unconditional love in great waves. He had breathed the Word of the Divine into their consciousnesses. It flowed without ceasing. It soaked into every pore and atom of these noble friends.

*And the light that shines beyond the sky,
On top of all,
On every height,
In the highest worlds beyond which

There is no higher.
That light
Is the same as the light
In the heart of man
Beautiful to see
And of great renown is he
Who knows this,
Who knows this!

The night was quiet and still and whispered without ceasing, rolling out its most hidden secrets to all whose hearts were open.

Slowly but surely, the deep blue of night gave way to a silken orange and turquoise glow. Stars gently faded into emptiness and the sweet crescent moon drew a veil across her face as the mighty sun rose in warm resplendance. The rays stretched gradually across to the carriages of the train, warming the companions and arousing them from their slumber, thus slowly awakening them to the new day. One by one, they stayed just where they were perched, listening to the continual lyrical song of the train. *Chug-a-dug-a, chug-a-dug-a, chug-a-dug-a, chug-a-dug-a.*

It was as if Alokah's dream were true. They were indeed being looked after by a great and loving Presence that manifested itself in the form of the beautiful spirit eagle who wove a connecting thread of love and light uniting them all.

Ajitah, aware of her duties as a co-leader, started to sing her song.

I am the Mystic Lover
I call to your honey-filled heart
May you become intoxicated
May you play your part.

Ananta stretched out his wings and nuzzled his beak on Ajitah's cheek.

'Umm, I love you,' she said.

'I love you too, my dearest,' replied Ananta as he surveyed her little face. 'Now we must play our part and have a word with the others. Let's see who's awake.'

Gradually, all the friends woke up and proceeded to stretch their wings.

'Good morning, good morning, everybody. How are you all today?' asked Ananta. All responded with various positive grunts, whistles, peeps and croaks.

Ajitah carried on singing and in no time at all, the rest of the company had joined in.

I am the Mystic Lover
I call to your honey-filled heart
May you become intoxicated
May you play your part.

'Oh, yes, yes,' sighed Alokah. 'So beautiful, so very beautiful!'

The floor of their carriage was scattered with grain from the collapsed bags and the friends settled down to an early morning snack. Then Ananta and Ajitah suggested that they might all like to get together and discuss the next stage of the journey.

'Yes, let's do that,' agreed Adesah

'Good idea!' responded Ameya.

'We've got lots to share, too,' said Alokah and Agnivalah nodded his head in agreement.

Amritah said, 'It is very important that we know what we are going to do when we reach *Katpadi Junction*. We must talk.'

Adinah agreed with her, 'Yes, we must.'

Abhilasha sighed. 'We must forget our worldly problems. We must discuss how we can achieve that, too.'

'That ith a difficult one, said Ameya, but 'I have tho many questionth contherning *who* I am, I don't know where to begin!'

At that moment a great shadow darkened the carriage and, for a second, nobody could see the others. At the same instant, a tantilising presence warmed each one of the friends and in came the great spirit eagle.

'Oh, Ameya, your friend has arrived,' whispered little Alokah. 'I'm so pleased!'

Ananta and Ajitah immediately welcomed him into their circle. All the companions could see him clearly now. There was such a tremendous force of Love emanating from his presence that nobody could resist it and his body seemed to glisten from an inner glow. Everyone had a smile on their face.

I come in peace to prepare and guide you all. I have spoken with Anadi, who lives at Arunachala. I believe that Amarah has already spoken to you of him. He paused.

'Ah, so you have heard of Anadi?' gasped Alokah.

Several others expressed amazement at the mention of his name.

'Yes,' he said.

Amritah then asked a question, 'Where

is Arunachala?'

Arunachala is the Holy Hill that rises out of the plains. It is your destination. It is the Hill of your dreams. It is the Hill of fire and Love. Lord Shiva has made himself manifest in the form of this Hill as the Supreme and Unmoving Teacher. There used to be a Wise One who lived there. The Holy Hill was his teacher. He lived constantly in a state of Spontaneous Presence in the Divine Self all the time. His name was Bhagavan Ramana. Although he died quite a long time ago, his spirit is still there. Many have seen him in his spirit form and experienced his love. You may meet him if you are very lucky. He loved birds. He once had a crow that would not leave him alone. It followed him when he went on his walks on the Holy Hill. It is buried at the foot of the Hill.

All the other birds turned to look at Ameya who was clearly thrilled to hear these words.

Then the divine spirit eagle began to sing. His voice was unearthly and blissful. If The

Nine could have *seen* the song, they would have seen many brilliant rainbows dancing in the atmosphere all around them.

And the light that shines beyond the sky,
On top of all,
On every height,
In the highest worlds beyond which
There is no higher.
That light
Is the same as the light
In the heart of man
Beautiful to see
And of great renown is he
Who knows this,
Who knows this!

Light and beauty radiated and encircled this wonderful fellowship. Each companion was raised to a higher vibration of thinking, of being, as every utterance of this divine melody plucked at the strings of their eager hearts. Each one of the friends becoming as One, inseparable and eternal. Many minutes passed in the stillness after the end of this song. Time stood still in an eternal moment.

Chapter Twenty-four

Once again, the spirit eagle spoke: *I will tell you something. It may answer some of your questions. It is a teaching from a long time ago. A very famous Sage called Vasishta was discussing with Lord Rama. This is what he said:*

Listen carefully: *"I am the space, I am the sun. I am the directions, above and below. I am the gods. I am the demons. I am all beings, I am darkness, I am the earth, the oceans ... I am the dust, the wind, the fire and all this world. I am omnipresent. How can there be anything other than Me? If you adopt this attitude you will rise beyond joy and sorrow ... the Self alone is the light in all things in the world, though they (the things) are in fact false.

At all times, everything is known only by direct experience. Whatever is experienced and known here in this world, all that is the Self. ... (which is) devoid of the duality of the experiencing and the experience. It is the Self alone that exists everywhere at all times, but because of its extreme subtlety, it is not experienced (by the senses) ... All activities take place in the light of the sun, but if the activities cease the sun does not suffer loss: even so, it is on account of the Self that the body functions, but if the body perishes, the Self does not suffer loss. The Self is not born, nor does it die, it does not acquire, nor does it desire, it is not bound, nor is it liberated ... Liberation is but a synonym for Pure mind, correct Self-knowledge and a truly awakened state ... "

Strive for this awareness my friends. You have a great chance before you. This is your destiny. Be true to yourselves and listen to your hearts. Listen to everything that is imparted to you. Meditate upon it and because of your experience, you will eventually be able to help others. The world needs you. Do your part.

When we reach Katpadi, I will guide you towards the Holy Hill of Arunachala. It is not so far, but it will take some time. It is hot here and I realise that you will need many stops to rest. I will be back soon. Away he flew.

The Nine sat for a long time in contemplation. Nobody moved. The sun had risen fully and the heat was beginning to tell on the friends.

'So Ramana had a crow friend? How lovely,' thought Ameya.

'How hot it is here,' said Adesah, as he fanned himself.

'Yeth, it ith very hot' said Ameya. Thoth of us who have black coat feel it a lot,' and he cast a glance at Abhilasha, whose coat was as black as coal.'

The friends were becoming thirsty.

'We must do something,' said Agnivalah.

Ananta and Ajitah looked at each other and Ajitah said, 'Let us sit down now and talk. We still have a long way to go and we cannot leave the train unless we want to fly the rest of the way. What do you want to do?'

Adinah suggested that as the train was going quite fast, it would be impractical to fly off and hope to catch it up. The rest of the company agreed.

Adesah had an idea, 'I could go up onto the roof of our carriage and see if I can see if I can move along the train and peek into the carriages and see what I can find.'

'That is a good idea,' agreed Ananta, 'I will come with you. Let's go now.' And before anyone could stop them, they had gone.

Ananta and Adesah flew quickly up onto the top of the train. It was quite windy there but not enough to blow them off. It was a bit risky but they just managed to keep standing. Gradually, they edged their way along the carriage tops and eventually reached the front of the train and the engine room. The driver was sitting there and was talking to a passenger who was asking him some questions. Our two friends listened hard and found out that they were only half an hour away from *Katpadi*. That was very good news! As they looked around, they noticed a bucket hooked to the wall with water in it. It was put there in case of fire. Ananta and Adesah looked quickly at each other, hopped down, then sat on the rim of the bucket and had a good drink. The water was a bit stale, but it was better than nothing. Then they quickly flew out and hopped carefully back to the others.

'Well, said Ananta, we shall reach *Katpadi* in about half an hour. It is not long to wait according to a conversation we overheard. But if you want a drink, there is water in a bucket beside the engine driver. It is quite windy outside and we would suggest that you go only if you are desperate.'

Adesah announced, 'If anyone wants to go for a drink, I will go with you.'

'That is kind, thank you,' said Abhilasha. 'I am very thirsty.'

'So am I,' repeated the others. So, slowly and very carefully, Adesah led them one by one along the tops of the carriages in the wind to the bucket in the engine room for a drink. None of them was noticed going to the bucket. They were very careful and quiet as they edged their way in. It wasn't until Agnivalah was having his drink, that the engine driver suddenly saw him and tried to catch him.

'Hey you! Good heavens! What kind of creature are you? Get out!' and with a lot of flapping and fluttering, he just managed to escape.

'What a terrible shock, it was, but I did manage to get a drink,' Agnivalah said as he breathlessly recounted his story.

Ajitah spoke, 'Dear Adesah, thank you so much for your kind help to us all. We couldn't have done it without you. Bless you.'

'We don't have too long to wait now. That is good,' said Adesah as he looked out into the distance.

Ananta and Ajitah called the group together. 'Let us have a quick consultation. We need to prepare ourselves now.'

Chapter Twenty-five

And so it was that the beloved friends had a chance to talk about the night and their dreams. They talked about the beautiful music that wafted in and out of their minds. They talked of their understanding of what the divine spirit eagle had shared with them. They talked of the luminous presence that had enveloped them. They talked of how peacefully they had slept. And they talked of how *loving* they all felt when they woke up. They opened their hearts to one another and all agreed that, yes, they felt that they were being watched over. They all felt safe. They discussed what they should do when they arrived in *Katpadi*.

'As soon as we arrive, I will go and see if I can make contact with my relative,' said Agnivalah.'

'But you can't go alone,' said Adinah, 'I shall come with you.'

'No, it is not neccessary for anyone to come with me. I wish to go alone. I will give out a call and see who comes. Don't be afraid for me. I will be fine.'

But no one could agree as to what to do or not to do, until Ajitah said, 'You know, I feel very strongly that we are all being looked after. We have come so far. It is not possible for us to fail now. Do not be disheartened because we have not agreed yet on a plan. My feeling is that when we arrive, we will be guided, but we must fly out of the station first, as quickly as possible, and find a shady place in which to discuss the next move. By then, maybe Agnivalah will have made contact with his relative. If not, I am sure we will find someone who is able to help us.'

'You are right,' said Amritah. The others agreed and Ananta and Ajitah ended the meeting with all of them singing:

I am the Mystic Lover
I call to your honey-filled heart

May you become intoxicated
May you play your part.

Peace had returned to the group.

Whilst the company were busily discussing what to do next, a stranger had joined them. He leant on a railing, quietly listening to their conversation. Nobody noticed him.

Eventually, a loud whistle made everyone jump. They had finally arrived at *Katpadi*.

'Hooray,' shouted Adesah, and up flew The Nine out of the station.

They looked around and found a shady, empty wall to sit on, well away from the crowds. Immediately, Agnivalah left to search for his relative. He was not alone: his wife's spirit had joined him. He felt so happy, so complete. As he flew, he began talking to his wife's spirit. 'Where shall we look first for our relative?'

Before she could reply, a voice behind them spoke. *Please come this way*. It was the stranger who had come on board the train. Agnivalah immediately turned round but could see no one behind him.

'How strange. What is going on? I cannot see you. Who are you?' He looked about him and then he saw an elderly man with a white beard standing on the road below him.

Agnivalah wasn't quite sure what to do and dithered for a few seconds, nearly falling to the ground before he saved himself.

Don't be afraid, I will show you the way, said the stranger.

At that, Agnivalah flew down to his feet and the kindly stranger bent over him, offering his arm. Agnivalah took the cue and jumped up. Very gently, the elderly man lifted him up and the two of them moved over to the side of the road.

Agnivalah listened intently as the stranger spoke very softly to him.

Go back to your friends and wait there with them. I will send someone directly to help you. You will not find your relative here. He has left the area.

Agnivalah was speechless. All he could do was a sort of bow. He bent his head in humility to this beautiful stranger who seemed to shine in the sunlight. He could sense something very wonderful about this man, but he couldn't quite explain it.

The stranger lowered his arm and Agnivalah hopped off and flew back to the wall near the station where he found the others.

The friends were very excited with his news and wondered who it could possibly have been.

'I hope my relative is all right,' pondered Agnivalah. 'Anyway, he may not have known the way to the Holy Hill. And as it turns out, we are being sent another guide. I really had no idea where to begin looking. I am most grateful to that kind stranger.'

Chapter Twenty-six

After some time, the shadow of the great spirit eagle descended and perched a little bit apart from the group.

Greetings, my friends. He turned towards Agnivalah and said, *I see you have already met my friend. I will take you all onwards so that you may fulfill your destiny. You all have a great capacity which you do not realise at the moment, but in due course, you will each come to know who you are and why you have been called.*

'Who is your friend?' asked Agnivalah.

The elderly eagle did not respond but continued talking.

Now, let us go forth. Follow me.

He rose up majestically into the sky. Everybody followed him. Up, up and up they flew. Past houses and trees, across valleys and plains.

Eventually, they all paused for a rest by a small stream near an old banyan tree. The eagle was obviously pleased that all had been able to keep up with him. He had done his best not to fly too fast. An even pace is what he maintained and everyone appreciated it.

'Thank you. Thank you for guiding us,' said Ananta. 'We are so grateful to you.'

'We would never have survived without your help,' piped up Ajitah. 'Thank you, O Wise One.'

You are welcome. Stay here for the rest of the day, relax and do whatever you wish, but be prepared and ready to depart when Anadi arrives at night fall.

I must leave you now. May you find what you are seeking. You are approaching the Divine Source. In a short time, you will reach the end of your journey. Then the great spirit eagle began to sing:

Divine Souls, I speak to your Heart
You, a shining Light must impart

218

The Wisdoms that soon you will own
By God's hand will be shown
Rest awhile beside this brook
And nurture Love within your look
Never sing a song that hurts a soul
Only Divine Rhapsodies to make one whole
You, the beloved seekers of God.

As soon as he had finished his song, he spread out his huge wings and flew away into the distance. All eyes were glued upon him until he could no longer be seen.

Nobody found their voice for quite some time. The little stream sparkled in the sunlight and tinkled past them with a refreshing gurgle. Considering how hot it was, there was still a good amount of water running through and it seemed to speak to them as they sat in the silence.

'You, the mystic birds...sing, sing, sing your love song.'

Each blessed bird sat quietly and absorbed the sweet sound. It refreshed and gladdened their spirits. It lightened their burdens. It even felt as if it was washing away all their pains and sadnesses. The sound was the music of the spheres to these divine souls.

'We have been given so much,' said Ajitah, finally. 'What a gift! Now we must wait for Anadi. I am so very happy that we have reached this far. I love you all. Thank you for being here. Perhaps we could have a gathering together and share our feelings? What do you think, my friends?'

'Why, yes, it would be a lovely thing to do,' agreed Amritah.

The rest of the company quickly moved closer to the stream. They formed a little huddle under the spreading tree. It was cool here and nobody would have been able to see them without really looking hard, but they may well have heard them as they joyfully sang their unifying song:

I am the Mystic Lover
I call to your honey-filled heart

May you become intoxicated
May you play your part.

Ananta spoke up, 'We have been through a lot together. We are nearly at the end. There is no going back for any of us. We are not the same as we were when we first left our homes. I am certainly pleased that Ajitah and I both decided to come on this quest. I know, from my side, that I will never look back with regret at my life or wish that it had been lived in any other way. To me, this is the most important journey anyone can ever make ... the journey to the divine Source. Thank you everyone for loving us.' There was a pause, then he asked, 'How do you all feel?'

Agnivalah offered to share his thoughts: 'First of all, I would like to thank Adinah for suggesting that we follow the train routes. To ride on the trains was a clever idea. It has saved us a lot of time and who knows what difficulties. I am very impressed with how we have all coped with the discomforts of travelling in this unusual fashion. Finding food and water has not always been easy. There have been many stops on the way and we have not always found a comfortable spot, but no-one has ever uttered a cross word to another. This, to my mind, is remarkable. I respect you all deeply.' Then he gave a little bow to the company. 'I have been blessed by having my beloved wife's spirit with me all the way. Her presence has helped me enormously. I have also enjoyed the discussions we have shared together and I am beginning to understand more about living in the present moment and to appreciate the *now*. I feel nothing but gratitude for being here. Thank you my dear friends.' Then he bowed once more.

'What a gracious bird,' thought Amritah.

'Thank you, dear Agnivalah for sharing with us,' said Ajitah.

Adinah was the next to speak, 'Thanks for your kind words Agnivalah. I have to say that I don't think I could have made this journey if I had had to fly all the way. I am too old for long flights now. I was very happy that you were all so enthusiastic to travel by this way. Nobody has got sick either, which is a good thing. We have all kept pretty cheerful. I was very grateful to you Adesah, when I had some doubts as to whether I could make the journey or not, because you said that if I had a strong wish to go, then of course I would be able to make it. You don't know how much that advice has kept me going along the way. Thank you very much.' He bowed, 'I cannot believe that we are nearing the very end of our journey. The next step is not going to be easy for any of us. This is going to be our biggest test. My wish is that we shall all arrive safely at our destination. During the journey, I have been accompanied, on and off, by the *Wise One* who initiated me a long time ago up in the Himalayas. He has been a great source of strength to me. I am very grateful for that. I think that we are all being protected in so many ways, otherwise we would never have got this far. Thank you all, dear companions for being my friends.' So saying, he bowed very low to everyone.

'Thank you dear Adinah for your kind words and love,' said Ananta.

Next, Abhilasha spoke up and said, 'This journey has changed me so much. I am grateful to you Amritah for all the support you have given me. There was no way I could have made it emotionally had it not been for your time and kindness. I thank you sweet angel and you too, dear Ameya for coming with me. I appreciate your friendship very much. I know that I haven't always been very nice to you and so I wish to say sorry to you. I would never want to upset you.' She gave him such a warm, sunny smile that it took Ameya completely by surprise. He blushed but could say no more.

'I haven't got much else to say,' said Abhilasha, 'except that I want to tell you all that I am so pleased that I have made it this far. I thank you all,' and she bowed to the group.

Then Ameya responded with a little laugh, having composed himself after Abhilasha's apology.

'Ha ha, thanks for wanting me to come with you dear Abhilasha. All ith forgiven.
I know that you don't really mean half of what you thay. You have a good heart, and I think it

ith even more beautiful than it wath before we thet out.' He nodded his head and smiled towards her, 'I am very happy to have joined thith group. You have thuch warm heartth. I have learned tho much and have felt very thupported on tho many levelth. I am eternally grateful that I have come and thank you both Ajitah and Ananta for being such good and thoughtful leaders.'

'Oh Ameya, you are so sweet and good,' said Ajitah. 'Thank you for sharing. Yes Adesah, I see you that you would like to speak now.'

Adesah was bouncing up and down, 'Yes please. I have been thinking a lot in my quiet moments about what Amarah said concerning Love being the key and the need to give out Love willingly. That thought has really helped me. I actually *do* feel happy and full of love. Love for everybody and everything. It is quite remarkable. I feel that I have changed for the better. You have all been terrific company to travel with and helpful too. Thank you Alokah and Agnivalah for joining me on this trip. I might not have been brave enough to come alone.' He bowed.

'Thank you dearest Adesah for sharing your thoughts and for keeping us cheery all the way here,' smiled Ananta.

Alokah spoke next, 'I have always believed that we would reach our destination. Thank you both Agnivalah and Amritah for your special love. I am so glad you are here to share all this too. We are not there yet though, but we are close. We have certainly been protected by many divine beings. I would never have been able to travel this distance without all your love and support for me. I know that we can achieve this last lap now if we all continue to help each other. Good luck everybody and thank you, dear friends.'

'Oh, dearest Alokah,' said Amritah. 'We have all benefited from your words of wisdom and humility. I also thank you two love birds: you are very precious.'

Ajitah thanked Alokah for her kind words and the company for opening their hearts.

226

The beloved friends ended their little consultation with some heartfelt singing.

I am the Mystic Lover
I call to your honey-filled heart
May you become intoxicated
May you play your part.

The Nine grew quiet and thoughtful. The mid-afternoon sun was high in the sky. There was not so long to wait now. The stream continued to whisper her song to the company.

You, the mystic birds ... sing, sing, sing
your love song.

Chapter Twenty-seven

The Nine gradually drifted away from the circle and went in search of a quiet corner. All went first to the stream for a drink. Several flew up into the branches of the tree. Now was an opportunity to have some rest, to take a little time for reflection, to gather their thoughts for the onward journey and to renew their strength. Time to find some food and to bathe. Yes, a time for understanding and innerstanding.

Much later on, as the sun lowered towards the horizon, a song could be heard in the distance calling out ...

My hearing, sight, my tongue and hand:
all He.
Then I am not, for all that is, is He.
I think I am, and thought is but a dream.
When I awake, all that remains is He.

It was very faint at first and only one heard it, Alokah. She was alert in a second, listening and listening in case it came again.

A few minutes later, again it was heard: this time a little closer.

Ananta and Ajitah fluttered down out of the tree at the same time: 'Did you hear that?' they spluttered together.

The song could now be heard a little nearer. It was still a long way off, but the rest of the company had heard the faint call.

'That must be Anadi,' whispered Amritah. Her heart started beating very fast.

'Oh, I am so excited. Where is he? Where is he?' squeaked Abhilasha.

Again, the song was repeated. Now everyone was very excited and waited and waited for the next call. They did not have long to wait, for the call was very close now. It was the sweetest, most fragrant, divine song any of them had ever heard. Whoever was singing was almost upon them.

Finally, the song came from the very

top of their tree. The blessed company did not, could not move. They simply stared up into the branches as they tried to see who had arrived.

Anadi, the spiritual brother of Amarah had arrived. Here was the one that Amarah had told them to expect towards the end of their journey. He had then explained to The Nine that Anadi lived on the Holy Hill in the South. He was eternal. In fact his name meant just that. He was a great and generous soul, who would enable them all to understand the truth of their very existence and would offer much help to them so that they might fulfil their destiny and thereafter become a source of strength to others in these difficult times.

The company continued to stare. They could not see the singer yet, but all could feel his presence.

Anadi flew straight down and sat with the friends. He was a nightingale. All gathered around and waited in silence for him to speak. Of noble bearing, he emanated a divine luminous presence. Here sitting before them all, was a warm-hearted, good-humoured, caring and wise being. He commanded immediate respect and trust. They began to relax just a little.

Anadi surveyed them all. He cast a glance at each one for a few seconds and it seemed as if he was looking into their very souls. Each one felt their heart-beat quicken as a soft, calm sense of peace pervaded their consciousness when his eyes met theirs. All this time, not a word was spoken. The energy around the place was electrifying. Nobody moved. For a long time they bathed in his presence. It was as if they had become rooted there for ever.

Eventually, Anadi, the nightingale of Paradise, addressed the company:

Dearly beloved friends. You have come a long way. Each of you has been called to undertake this journey. You are all very blessed and have sacrificed your former lives to seek out the Truth. You have done well, my friends. Without knowing it, each one of you has passed into the Divine Realms. You have come through the Valley of Search. Your hearts have been awakened to the call. You have journeyed into the Valley of Love. You have passed through the Valley of Knowledge and discovered the veiled mysteries in your hearts. You have passed through the Valley of Unity and found the oneness of true friendship there.

* "...A pure heart is as a mirror; cleanse it with the burnish of love and severance from all save God, that the true sun may shine within it and the eternal morning dawn. Then wilt thou clearly see the meaning of "Neither doth My earth nor My heaven contain Me, but the heart of My faithful servant containeth Me."

You have entered the Valley of Contentment and have felt the divine breezes awakening your hearts. You have travelled far. You have turned away from the things of the world. The burning fire of divine Love has seized your hearts and you, the lovers, are calling out to the Beloved.

Then Anadi sang a beautiful note:

**Only heart to heart can speak
The bliss of mystic knowers;

233

No messenger can tell it
And no missive bear it.

There was a short pause before he continued,

Now you are poised on the brink of the Valley of Wonderment. Life is a mystery to be unravelled. Search and search and search again for your hearts to fully awaken. You have all yet to reach the end of your journey. None will be disappointed. To pass through the final Valley of True Poverty and Absolute Nothingness, every single thing has to be surrendered, even your identities. This may be a little difficult for you to grasp, and may seem even frightening, but when you come to realise that you are not your bodies or senses and you are not your names, but that you are Absolute Pure Love, you will die to your self and live in your true Self. Do not worry that you do not understand this yet. All things will be revealed when your hearts have become truly pure. That is why you have chosen to come. This is your destiny. If you reach the ultimate goal of the last Valley, you will be able to help many other beings. This is my message.

I will now sing for you a song from Arunachala, the Sacred Holy Hill. Then, if you have any questions we will share them together.'

He sang with great feeling:

*In the Heart, thou dost dance as 'I', as the Self, O Lord, they call Thee by the name 'Heart'.

In that sacred place, nobody spoke. Only the sound of the little stream could be heard.

'You, the mystic birds...sing, sing, sing your love song.'

Anadi looked around him at the circle of beloved friends. All had their eyes closed. They were in the bliss of the Self, the Divine. the Heart. Each one, he could see, had been touched by his words. Those sacred words of all the Divine Teachers who had come down the ages to teach unconditional Love to those whose hearts are ever open and waiting.

Now, his job was to lead them all to the

Holy Hill, Arunachala.

Eventually, the divine company opened their eyes and all attention was fixed on that divine soul, Anadi. As he surveyed these wondrous birds, he saw the light of truth shining in their eyes. He knew, yes, he *knew* without a doubt, that these were noble souls.

No one had any questions. For how could they speak after that delicious outpouring of sanctity and love?

Now we must leave this place to complete the journey. Follow me.

Chapter Twenty-eight

It was dark. The evening had turned to full-blown night. The Nine felt uplifted and spellbound as they rose into the air. This was pure magic. No thoughts for past events, just flying into the *now*.

Ameya found himself feeling that he was living very much in the *now* as he soared up on the wing. He felt free, yes, free. Even his lisp seemed to have disappeared or was it his imagination?

Anadi, ahead of The Nine, seemed to glow. He positively shone. All the company could see his wings shine as they spanned out, reaching for the Holy Hill. The flight would take them most of the night.

Ananta was thinking to himself as he rose into the air with Ajitah at his side, 'This feels like we are the True Lovers that we both dreamed about. It feels like it's even more than just that. It feels like all of us are the True Lovers of the Divine Self.

Ajitah was right beside Ananta. She could feel the wind ruffle her feathers as he beat his wings up and down. She smiled to herself and thought about how much they loved each other. She was so lucky to have such a beautiful soul as a husband. Now, they were going to the very Hill that they had both dreamed about: how amazing. Then, she heard a voice which seemed to come from all around,

You, the divine Lovers seek for the Beloved and you think you are going somewhere. There is nowhere to go for one is within the other already.

'Did you hear that?' whispered Ananta.

'Yes, yes, my dearest. It sounds like the voice of our dream,' responded Ajitah.

'It is always within us,' exclaimed Ananta. 'I understand now. When I look at you,

I see the Beloved. The Beloved is to be seen everywhere and anywhere. We do not have to *go* anywhere. Do you get it?

Ajitah said, 'Oh, yes, yes, dearest, I think I understand it too. Oh, oh, so divine.'

On they all flew, following Anadi in the light of his own bliss. He lit up the sky with his brightness. The night air was cool as they all stretched out their wings. They were on the homeward run now and all were happy.

Agnivalah and Alokah were flying side by side.

'Agnivalah, Agnivalah, can you hear me?, Alokah called out. 'I can see that we are all linked together by a golden thread. Can you see it?'

Agnivalah looked towards her briefly, 'You know, I can! Well I'll be blessed! That is amazing. We are very fortunate, *Alokah*.'

Alokah said, 'I can see your dear wife

beside you, too. She is connected to the thread and so is Anadi. It is a sign, I'm sure. We are so very blessed.'

Amritah was accompanied by Abhilasha on one side and Ameya on the other.

Ameya spoke out, 'I cannot believe how fortunate we all are. I am so grateful to be here as one of the companions.'

'Hey, did you hear that?' said Abhilasha. 'You've lost your lisp Ameya. How did you do that? And do you know, I am feeling so full and free. I have never felt like this before. There is something going on, don't you think?'

Ameya responded, 'I don't know how, but my lisp has totally gone. I feel so clear inside. Not fuzzy any more. It is a miracle. What do you think of that Alokah?'

'Yes, you have lost your lisp. I am very happy for you dear Ameya. And now we are all flying towards our destiny. It feels like things are beginning to happen already, doesn't it? I feel that my dearest uncle Raji-B is with me too. It's like he is right here beside me, encouraging me. Oh, I don't know quite what is happening, but it seems that this is the extraordinary event that my parents envisaged for me when I was small. They always thought that I was destined for something good, although they were never quite sure what. I feel clear and I feel so much love surrounding me. Can you feel it too?'

Abhilasha answered, 'Yes, I can feel a tremendous love. It looks like there is a white haze embracing us all which must be all that light that is shining from those wings of Anadi. He is very bright, isn't he? And do you know, I don't feel tired at all.'

Last but not least came two more friends, Adesah and Adinah.

'This flight will be my last, said Adinah. I feel it in my old bones. Yet strangely enough, I am beginning to feel rather like a young parrot again. I am not tired at all.'

Adesah said, 'You are looking great

too, exactly like a young parrot,' and he laughed. Then he added, 'What an opportunity this journey has been for us all. I wouldn't have missed this for the world. I am so grateful that my friends, Alokah and Agnivalah came along too. I might not have come otherwise.'

And so the conversations between the friends came and went. As they flew on, something began to happen. They started feeling a lightness of being. Yes, they felt lighter and brighter. On and on they flew. They melted one into the other. The gentle breeze of the night was all around them. It felt as if they were really only one large bird flying, instead of lots of separate ones. The sensation was astonishing. Eventually, as they were flying across the plain, a dark, mountainous shape loomed ahead.

'That must be the Holy Hill ahead, Arunachala,' Adesah said excitedly, to Alokah and Agnivalah.

'Umm, ah yes ...'

That was the last utterance heard between the three friends. All became silent. Only the whooshing of their beating wings could be heard.

As they flew, another joined them: the beautiful golden spirit eagle with divine light in his eyes.

The Holy Hill Arunachala
Tiruvannamalai
South India

Chapter Twenty-nine

Night faded and the early morning sky paled into a soft pink and orange dawn. The sun rose, reflecting myriad hues as the shadows ran away. The Holy Hill was ablaze with the early morning sunlight. Up and up and up ascended The Nine with their escorts until they reached a small cave with a tree outside it, on the side of the Hill. The stranger that Agnivalah had met on the train was sitting there in peace and quiet. Here sat Bhagavan Sri Ramana Maharshi.

Agnivalah was so happy to meet the stranger and immediately went up to him and sat at his feet. He felt such a love emanating from this being. He felt that he wanted to stay there for ever.

Following his lead, the other birds all crowded around Bhagavan and he began feeding them with all kinds of soft grains. They had never before tasted such heavenly morsels. Each was fed by Bhagavan's own loving hand.

Alokah went up to their guide and said, 'Dearest Anadi, you have been so kind to us. You have brought us safely here. We wish to thank you from the bottom of our hearts.'

'Yes, oh yes, thank you so very much. You are a great and wise leader. We love your song. How can we learn to sing like you?' asked Amritah.

And so it was that Anadi began to sing:

Before language was
Silence is.
This our natural state:
Spontaneous Presence.

He continued, *Dearly beloved friends. You are at the entrance to the final Valley of your search. You are at the feet of the Beloved. Rest awhile. Breathe here. Live and love here. Your hearts are open. Fill them with nectar. Die to the self and live in the Self. Realise who you are. To learn how to sing, you must become silent. You will hear much from within when your mind is stilled. Be content. Listen, listen to the song of the Heart, then you will finally be able to sing.*

All sat in the bliss of the presence. The song wove its magic into all their hearts. Anadi's song was divine.

As they sat, the Hill became luminous. Bhagavan was luminous, Anadi and the glorious spirit eagle were luminous. They could see light radiating and dancing about their being. The birds felt as if they were becoming light beings. Their personalities, their sense of separation as they had always known it, started to drop away. Their desires and their longings dissolved into a vast luminous feeling of Love. It was all-encompassing. It was supreme.

Long they remained in this peaceful state, listening to the music of the spheres. Their minds became lighter and lighter. Time passed. The days passed, the nights came and went, yet on they sat. They remained resting in their Heart space. Their coloured feathers took on a translucent hue of the Divine. All fear was gone and all attachment had disappeared. Their little ego personalities, their ordinary consciousnesses had become drowned in a vast expanse of Pure, Divine Love which enveloped them all.

Then the great spirit eagle began to sing out to the world. He sang of the greatness that the blessed companions had reached:

'Pure love has come dancing, alone and quiet.
Sitting within their own luminous nature.
In the bliss of the In-lightened Heart of the Self,
Spontaneous Presence.
Dissolution of ebb and flow within the Source.
That unique underlying state
Whereby ordinary consciousness
And Supreme consciousness dissolve,
Merging one into the arms of the other.
The falling away of desires,
Of wishes to be fulfilled and
Of attachments to outcomes.
Freed of confines and definitions of duality,
And to be free of hopes and fears.
Spontaneous Presence, the Self,
Is the unifying Source of all.
It is total and uncompromising.

Doing or non-doing,
Coming and going is already fulfilled.
Leave things as they are, to
Come and go just as they please,
Like passing clouds in a clear blue sky.
Nothing is required
And there is nothing to be done.
There is no 'other',
For who can give and to whom,
If there is no one to receive?
And who can receive
If there is no one to give?
What is there that can be given or received
If there is only Spontaneous Presence?
Therefore, as Spontaneous Presence,
Dance the Eternal Present.
No judging,
No resisting,
No division,
For all is resolved in
Spontaneous Presence.
This has been none other
Than the fulfilment of their lives,
To rest eternally
In the In-lightened Heart.

And so it was, that the company of The Nine finally reached their destination. All would become great teachers of Wisdom in due course and many beings would be helped as a result of their epic journey.

Dear reader, back at Virbhadra in Rishikesh, birds still gather at the Asvatthah tree and at dusk you may hear them sing of The Nine who bravely left their home to answer the Call of the Divine and become One in the Divine Self.

Notes

Pg 43.   *The '*Bhagavad Gita*'(which means "Song of God") is probably the best known of the ancient holy scriptures of Hinduism. It is part of the '*Mahabharata*', a great Indian epic. There is a story that the *Asvatthah* tree is special because it has its roots in the heavens and its trunk and branches extending downwards to the earth, thus linking Heaven and Earth. This tree is known variously as 'The tree of life', 'The tree of knowledge', 'The tree of speech' or 'The world tree'. This is due to the fact that the tree is so ancient and considered a gift from the gods to infant humankind to guide and protect them. The tree was almost always depicted being guarded by a dragon or serpent. In ancient times the serpent represented wisdom. These were guardians who allowed no-one who had not first conquered their lower nature, to eat of the tree's fruits.

Pg 73, 143, 171   *Poem written by the 15th century Sanskrit poet, Kalidasa.

Pg 95, 174 *Mystical Poems of Rumi – A.J. Arberry 1968.

Pg 97   * Baha'u'llah.

Pg 101   *Swami Ram Das.

 Pg 197, 204   *Chandogya Upanishad (111,13,7) translation taken from 'The Hill of Fire' Monica Bose pg 121 Orchid Press, Bangkok 2002.

Pg 205 *The Supreme Yoga, (pg 308) Swami Venkatesananda.

Pg 229   *Baba Afzal Kashani

Pg 233   *Hadith: action or utterance traditionally attributed to the Prophet Muhammad or to one of the holy Imams.)

Pg 233   **Arabian Poem from The Seven Valleys and the Four Valleys (pg 30) Baha'u'llah

Pg 235   Bhagavan Sri Ramana Maharshi Hymn of Five Verses to Arunachala

Pg 238   Unknown.

All other quotes are by the author.

For further information visit www.advaitaspirit.org

Lightning Source UK Ltd.
Milton Keynes UK
04 December 2009

147070UK00002B/5/P

9 781849 232371